Dearest Jillian,
    Thank you for the name
(though the character who
bears it is no reflection of you)
and mostly, for sharing
the real-life adventure!
                    Love,
                    Gretchen

the

f r u i t

cocktail

diaries

Jill,
    Lets get back to New Orleans
real soon.
                    Love,
                    Brian

Brian Carmody
&
Gretchen Hayduk

the

cocktail

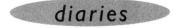

A Novel

St. Martin's Press • New York

Photo p. xii: Copyright MTA. Used by permission.

Photo p. 89: "Anxiety Quiz" from *What You Can Change and What
You Can't* by Martin E. P. Seligman, Ph.D. Copyright 1993 by Martin
E. P. Seligman, Ph.D. Reprinted by permission of Alfred A. Knopf,
Inc.

Photo p. 156: "Crazy Times." Copyright 1993 by The New York
Times Company. Reprinted by permission.

Photos by Luke Eder

Design by Junie Lee

Library of Congress Cataloging-in-Publication Data

Carmody, Brian.
    The fruit cocktail diaries / Brian Carmody and Gretchen Hayduk.
        p.   cm.
    ISBN 0-312-11796-5
    I. Hayduk, Gretchen.   II. Title.
    PS3553.A743F78   1995
    813'.54—dc20   94-24618
                                                    CIP

First Edition: January 1995
10 9 8 7 6 5 4 3 2 1

To Staś, who can't believe things take so long, and to my
family, who knows they just do.

—G. H.

To
Peter G.
and
my music-loving mom

—B. C.

I was walking on St. Marks Place one night, and it seemed as if the entire street had become a huge yard sale. Tons of other people's possessions were spread out on the sidewalk on dirty blankets and flattened cardboard boxes. It was the commonest of all flea markets—junk found in garbage cans or Dumpsters, or stolen from who knows where, was sprawled all over. It was the living example of "one person's garbage is another person's treasure."

I spied the first one between a half-empty bottle of perfume and a cracked teapot. One of those cloth-covered books that people write in, with bright fruit printed on both the front and back. I picked it up expecting it to be blank. When I saw the writing inside I quickly shut it. "Invasion of privacy," flashed through my mind. I bought it anyway. When I got home, the urge to read it was strong, but my conscience was stronger. The book sat untouched on my bedroom windowsill for days; its crazy fruit cover flirted with me daily, almost begging me, it seemed, to read it.

Three weeks to the night that I bought the diary, my resistance was beginning to crumble. I decided that in order to protect the author's secrets from myself, I would return the book to the East Village sidewalk where I had found it. That's when I found the second one. There on the same street, in the exact same spot, in that haven of clutter and disorder, lay another book identical to the one I had purchased weeks before. Two fruit cocktail diaries. "What are the chances?" I thought to myself. I bent down to have a look inside. Different handwriting. The plot thickened. What *were* these diaries? Were they somehow connected? Had the authors bought the books together? Were they friends? Lovers? Did they even know each other? Or was this all one big New York coincidence? Suddenly returning the original book was out of the question—I bought the second diary and raced back to my apartment. That night, sleep didn't stand a chance against my nosiness. I began reading, alternating from one book to the next (it was a pattern I would keep the whole way through). It wasn't long before I realized they *were* connected, only the diarists didn't know. The books became my secret refuge. Every Friday night alone, every slow moment at work, every pause in life led me back to their pages. Those anonymous lives sometimes seemed more real than my own. I began daydreaming about *him* and *her*. Where were they now, and what were they doing? I often wonder if they ever wonder where their diaries wound up.

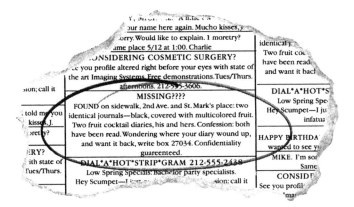

Y, MICHAEL. A little ...
our name here again. Mucho kisses, ...
orry. Would like to explain. 1 moretry?
same place 5/12 at 1:00. Charlie

CONSIDERING COSMETIC SURGERY?
See you profile altered right before your eyes with state of
the art Imaging Systems. Free demonstrations. Tues/Thurs.
afternoons. 212-555-3606.

MISSING????
FOUND on sidewalk, 2nd Ave. and St. Mark's place: two
identical journals—black, covered with multicolored fruit.
Two fruit cocktail diaries, his and hers. Confession: both
have been read. Wondering where your diary wound up,
and want it back, write box 27034. Confidentiality
guareenteed.

DIAL*A*HOT*STRIP*GRAM 212-555-2438
Low Spring Specials. Bachelor party specialists.
Hey Scumpet—I just ... sion: call it

---

identical j
Two fruit co
have been read
and want it bacl

DIAL*A*HOT*S
Low Spring Spe
Hey Scumpet—I ju
infatua

HAPPY BIRTHDA
wanted to see yo
MIKE. I'm sor
Same

CONSIDE
See you profil
'ma

---

sion; call it

told me you
kisses, J.
pretty?

ERY?
ith state of
Tues/Thurs.

the

fruit

cocktail

diaries

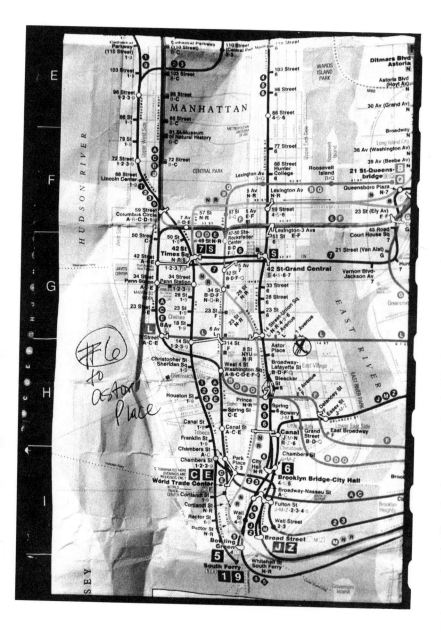

I've decided to unpack my bathroom tonight while listening to my old Partridge Family albums. It's supposed to take my mind off the fact that it's New Year's Eve in New York, and here I am—alone.

I dig through contents of boxes I don't even remember packing and find some old beauty supplies that I saved ages ago from college (and I swear they might even be leftovers from high school). Why I bothered to bring them along is a mystery to me.

I notice an apricot facial scrub with matching peel-away mask and decide to indulge; I pull back my hair from my face, feeling like the Noxema model whose face I once coveted. (The Partridges are singing, *"Believe me, I only wanna make you happy, so if you say, hey, go away, I will . . ."*)

I open the jar of scrub and there is a neon orange blob growing in one spot on the otherwise beige surface. I sniff it—nothing. This must be the "apricot" portion of the scrub gone bad, and I have half a notion to scoop out some of the untainted scrub anyway (like how you *can,* if desperate, pull off the moldy portion of bread and eat the rest).

How desperate am I?—I throw the scrub away. I do give in to the peel-away mask, however. (It *looks* okay, even though it has the consistency of rubber cement. Some strange sensorial memory assures me this is "normal.")

I am standing alone in my torn-apart bathroom, with cold, clammy guck pulling at my facial pores, with the stereo blaring, *"I think I love you—isn't that what life is made of,"* when something happens.

I look at the uneven pattern of the tiles in a bathroom I don't even feel right in yet, and realize that these old cosmetic souvenirs are somehow remnants of who I was and what I wanted to be.

What have I done? Packed a bunch of moldy cosmetics as a keepsake of a life I've thrown away? I'm not sorry that I decided to quit my promising advertising career back in Ohio, but what do I expect to find here instead? What are you supposed to do when you wake up one morning in the midst of all your superb goals and accomplishments and realize you've never gone after anything *real* in your entire life? This?

The edges of the mask on my face are drying and curling up; the needle on the record is stuck in the groove at the end of the song.

It's midnight. I want more.

I have in my life done many things which I am told I was not supposed to do. I have shied away and even run from things that give off the slightest scent of order and normality. And now here I am on the third day of a brand new year and, man, am I tired.

I admit I've slid by with little effort, up until now. And it's been easy. Being stupid is easy. My mind has been on nothing but my dick and the next place I was going to put it. I have spent the last five years of my life getting laid and going nowhere, and I've worked in just about every shitty restaurant on this crowded, hungry island, and it is no secret to anyone I wait on that I hate them. Chaos has kidnapped my mind and there is no one around to pay the ransom. The only thing I figure that I've *really* worked hard on is the accumulation of ex-boyfriends, and the numbers have gotten higher than I can count.

I see what's not right, and yet I have no clue as to what I should do. I know people see their therapists, and I no longer have such strong feelings against it. (On the contrary, it excites me to think of all those people seeing me go in and out of a shrink's office, wondering just how crazy I am.) But, because of my history of irresponsibility, I of course can in no way afford one of Freud's friends. So I am left with the wimpy little option of sorting out my head with my pen. Just how implausible this is, I don't know, but since it seems I don't know *anything* anymore, I figure it's worth a shot.

My new place is approximately twice the size of the walk-in closet of my apartment in Ohio. It doesn't really matter, though, because I don't have anything to put in it anyway. I only kept the table and chairs that Mom and Dad gave me ages ago. All the rest of my furniture I sold to pay for the Rent-a-Wreck to get here. I can't believe I didn't manage to save one penny of my steady salary while I was at the ad agency. Not one cent.

The last occupant left behind a futon which will work as a bed. It's barely thicker than a sleeping bag and I have no frame for it, so it's kind of folded up in one corner on the floor, like a strange, deflated beanbag chair.

I feel very comfortable here. On the mantle of the tiny teal-colored fireplace, I've placed all my seashells, dried flowers, and postcards that always looked like junk in my other place. Jeannie's black-and-white paintings actually complement these cracked, crooked walls.

My new neighborhood is a little on the scary side, though. All these drug dealers hang around all the time, muttering "smoke" and "sens" as you walk by. The first few times I heard them, I thought they were saying "smile" and "sex." Today, this crazy street person on St. Marks Place screamed at me to give him back his couch. If only he knew.

Cheryl from Ohio stopped by tonight. I used to work with her at the ad agency. She's in town for a Hidden Valley Ranch shoot, staying in one of the big midtown hotels. She brought along her brother Curt who lives on the Upper East Side and works for American Express. They just stood in my room, staring at the edge where the walls and ceiling come together as if it might cave in at any second. This got immediately boring and a bit embarrassing so I suggested we go out and get a cup of coffee.

Curt asked me if I was a Communist. I laughed that uncertain "This *is* a joke?" laugh and waited for his punchline.

Instead, Curt said that back when he was in college, a guy in his dorm had been a Communist and had moved all the furniture out of his room except the bare essentials—a mattress and a desk and a chair. He ended up getting kicked out of school—not because of his political preference, of course, but because he had moved university property without authorization.

I said that seemed drastic. Curt shrugged and said, "Rules are rules."

As they hailed a cab outside the coffee shop, the crazy guy who had yelled at me earlier walked by.

"Hey," he said, all tripped-out smiles now. "The couch . . . is cool."

"Yeah," I nodded back, smiling like we'd been best friends for years. "Just keep it. I don't need it anymore."

I think I surprised myself almost as much as Cheryl and Curt.

Tonight was my third double-shift in a row. Needless to say, I'm teetering ever so close to the brink. If I owe anything to my experiences as a waiter in New York, I guess it is that I now know how truly retarded humans can be.

"How firm is the meatloaf?"—what kind of question is that?

"You could sleep on it, asshole," I thought as I answered, "Extremely."

Meatloaf, spaghetti, veal scallopini—what does it matter? Why don't people just stay home and fix themselves those boil-in-bag dinners? True. I wouldn't have a job then, but I also wouldn't have a heart full of hate and a desperate need for a drink.

I applied for a job in a restaurant today because I have no money. I had to roll pennies to get some bills to buy subway tokens, since the subway-system people won't accept pennies. A very nasty bank teller wouldn't accept them either— what's going on? Did someone pass a law that I don't know about which made pennies obsolete? Finally, the guy at the corner deli where I get my coffee in the morning agreed to cash exactly two dollars' worth—but only after he saw that I was on the verge of tears.

I feel like I've been catapulted into another world where I am completely at the mercy of someone else's value system. I *thought* I knew how things worked. Suddenly I realize there's a whole other side I've never seen.

Like the dragon-lady manager at this restaurant where I applied. She looked at me like I was crazy when I told her I had waitressed on weekends in high school for a little extra spending money. (I remember how excited I'd been back then to get my first job and how much I secretly loved the little Swiss Miss uniforms we had to wear.) In *this* restaurant, I was informed, I'd have to wear an oxford shirt, khaki pants, and a man's tie. When I didn't object, she grudgingly told me I could trail for the job, and then, "We'd see."

I enthusiastically said, "Great!" but I am certain she is incapable of even cracking a smile. She just pulled out a wrinkled satin tie from behind the bar and handed it to me.

"See that you return this at the end of the shift."

Trailing, I found out later, consists of going through all the work of a regular shift but not getting paid for it. We followed the set-up waitress, Donna (a would-be Broadway singer who looks like Sandy Duncan), observing every move she made.

("Fork, fork, knife, spoon," Dragon Lady said as Donna placed each utensil on the linen napkins.) It was impossible to concentrate after almost an hour of this; I numbly nodded and replied "okay" to everything. From the look on Dragon Lady's face, I assume this was the wrong answer.

When the restaurant finally opened, she gave me a trial table to wait on, then she lurked two feet away to catch any mistake I made.

"Two pats of butter, not three," she reproached sharply, back at the wait station. "Let them *ask* if they want more."

As it got busier, she was forced to occasionally turn her eyes away from me. At these times, Donna whispered assorted information to me like, "Never let her catch you talking to other staff members," and "Paulo the night cook is *hot*," and "I just did a voice-over for a cartoon—wanna hear?"

As she was chirping away in some baby-seal voice, Dragon Lady snuck up from behind. Donna slid away, and I was left face-to-face with her. It was obvious she hated me; why didn't she just let me go *now*?

"Here are your shifts." She handed me a piece of paper. I just stared at her, my mouth open wide. "Get a tie and don't ever be late."

I can't believe it—I'm actually excited, even if the place is probably going to make me a nervous wreck. Why can't I squelch this thrill of anticipation? It's like the night before the first day of school when I was little. Why is this idiotic smile taking over my face? I'm still stymied at the thought of having to cash in more pennies to get a subway token to even get to this job tomorrow. I think:

MADWOMAN FORCES SMALL CHANGE ON MANHATTAN MERCHANTS

I was truly all set on being pissy and negative tonight. I was sure that I was completely bored with this city. There was absolutely not a thing worth doing, except maybe trying to be a pain in everybody's ass, including my own. I had no desire to go to a bar (imagine that), and no movie or book had even a chance of keeping me interested. So I fucked around in the apartment, trying desperately to bother Kevin, which I believe I did because he ended up throwing a copy of *British Vogue* at me. I have to admit I was stunned; Kevin may throw temper tantrums a lot, but throw a fashion magazine?—never! If our apartment was on fire, he'd rather barbecue his ass than leave his favorite *Harper's Bazaar* behind.

After he slammed his bedroom door, I decided it was time for me to subject the rest of the world to my mood. I checked my hair (which only made matters worse) and ventured out with no particular direction in mind. When I got outside, for some reason I looked up at the almighty heavens and witnessed something of a miracle. Up in the sky above 15th Street, there were five or six circles of light. I'm not talking Martian lights, just regular light lights. Like the kind of light that makes those search beams cross the sky every so often. Only these weren't searchlights. These were circles of light chasing each other across the New York night sky. Now I know that someone was at the other end of these things making them happen, and that made it all the more exciting to me. To know that it was someone's job to throw those lights up in the sky for whatever reason, well, shit, it made me smile and I believe I even got goosebumps. I would think I was crazy, if I wasn't already positive about it.

It just made me think. I bitch and moan, and I carry around all this crap all the time, never letting go of it, until it gets so close to me that it somehow gets inside me.

But now I'm FREE, HEALED, REPAIRED! And all because of some lights in the sky.

I went back inside where Kevin was still hermetically sealed in his room, so I got down on the floor and put my mouth under his door.

"I'm sorry, asshole," I whispered, and went in my room feeling like a better person.

Let's hope it lasts. At least until I wake up.

Last night my phone rang at three o'clock in the morning. An operator asked if I'd accept a collect call from Harold. Sure, why not? Except I don't know anyone named Harold.

"Miss ———?" this polite voice asked, badly mispronouncing my last name. "I wanted to let you know I just found your bank card."

This was too good to be true—I hadn't even realized it was lost, and here was some Good Samaritan looking out for me. I thanked him and said I'd cancel it right away.

"You know, it's really a hassle to have to get a new one," he said. "I can return it to you."

Even in my half-asleep state I recognized what a nice gesture this was.

He continued. "And maybe you wouldn't mind giving me a couple of bucks then? I'm kind of out of cash."

I felt the beginning of a warning signal going off in my brain, but he sounded so sincere—and sincere people can run out of money the same as shiftier types. I agreed to meet him somewhere in the morning.

"The thing is," he said, "it's freezing out here, and I could use some hot food right now."

Now? In the middle of the night? Did he think I was crazy?

"But it's three o'clock in the morning," I said.

"Exactly," he enthusiastically agreed, as if this were somehow a point in his favor, "and it's really cold."

"I'm sorry," I said. "I can't."

"That's okay," he said.

We hung up, but I couldn't get back to sleep. The wind seemed to be howling outside, and it occurred to me that a very decent-sounding person was spending the night in a horribly indecent way. Everybody knows you don't go out in the middle of the night to meet complete strangers, but I wondered—really, why *couldn't* I have done it?

I could have met him in one of the all-night diners around here—he still wouldn't have known where I lived. It would have been no more dangerous than going out with any other of my new acquaintances. How well do you really know anyone?

I was lying there getting really mad at my chickenshit self when the phone rang again. I accepted another collect call from Harold. I was so excited I'd been given a second chance that I didn't question why he called back. I suggested we meet right away at Veselka's on Second Avenue. I went through all my pockets, hoping to find a stray five, but came up only with the twenty I made at that horrible job today.

Clothes over pajamas, I walked out into the brisk air. It was darker on my street than I'd expected. Some big searchlights were cutting across the sky, making me feel like I was a refugee in some World War II movie.

When I turned the corner onto lit-up, gloriously populated Second Avenue, a tall, under-dressed guy stood waiting, and I knew it was Harold. All of a sudden, I was overcome with that feeling you get right before a blind date. He took a few steps toward me as I got closer.

"Miss ———?" he asked tentatively.

I told him to please, call me by my first name.

It felt like prom night.

He pulled my bank card out of his pocket as if it were a corsage. For his boutonniere, I handed him the twenty.

We stood there for a couple of minutes, shuffling our feet

and looking down at the ground. Finally I said I had to be
going, and he offered to walk me to my door.

"No, that's okay," I said, both of us aware of what was contained in that simple refusal.

When I went into work today, I had the intention of keeping my soul-saving experience to myself, but everyone was immediately suspicious of my cheerful mood. The manager pulled me aside and asked if I was stoned, and that's when I knew I couldn't stay quiet any longer.

Admittedly, I wasn't crystal-clear in the telling, and I couldn't find the right words to explain how seeing those lights made me feel, but all I got from those cretins were blank stares, rolled eyes, and a comment about me bumping my head. I just stood there and looked at everyone with my best "Don't you get it?" face. I tried discussing it with this waiter named Tony and all I got out of him was a bitchy "What's your point?"

I said I wasn't sure, "but haven't you ever been touched by something that you couldn't explain, but felt inside?"

He said, "Oh, you mean like seeing Patti LaBelle in concert?"

Hopeless queen.

At that point my joy had practically evaporated and I even felt somewhat embarrassed about spouting off like I had seen Jesus hovering over the Hudson or something.

Now I suppose I should have kept my little miracle to myself.

People aren't interested in what saves your soul; everyone's just looking to save themselves. Those lights, I'm afraid, were to most people just that—lights. So you live and learn. Miracles like everything else, I guess, only mean so much.

Apparently, in this business, it's not uncommon at all. Something just makes me feel funny about working at three different restaurants in two weeks' time. I've now reached the point that whenever I walk up Second Avenue, I have to cross the street back and forth to avoid passing in front of any of them.

I wish just one would have worked out. It's not that I wasn't catching on—every restaurant put me on their schedule; but the thought of those vulturous managers made me so nervous that when it came time for the first official shifts, I'd end up taking a long walk around Tompkins Square Park instead.

Here I am in the cold gray park again, watching two pigeons fight over one of those big pretzels.

I saw Joe tonight. He was walking toward me on Second Avenue. I saw him from a block away and he was wearing that annoying red coat and his Walkman. He didn't see me. It looked like he was lost in a song, and for some strange reason I didn't want him to see me. So I went into a deli and watched him walk by, singing away, having no idea I was there. I sort of laughed when I imagined what I would say if someone asked me what I was doing: "I'm hiding from my boyfriend."

Ain't love grand.

It's one of those rare, unseasonably warm, 60-degree days that seem to happen every January, everywhere. Coffee shops grab at the chance to open their sidewalk cafés, even for a day. It's an affirmation, it seems. Everyone's greedy for air and sunlight.

I'm eavesdropping again.

I guess it's a side effect of unemployment—some attempt to connect to the world in a way other than looking at the want ads.

A man and woman at the table next to me are very intelligently discussing sex. Freud's theories, the relationship to one's mother, and the fairy-tale marriage of the woman's brother are the topics that I've picked up so far.

I don't know why, but I like hearing about Mark (the woman's brother) and his wife, who lived in a little cottage when they reached that stage in their marriage where everything seems perfect. He was a fisherman then, I learn, and their daughter Jessica had just been born.

Then I guess I drifted off for a while because the next thing I hear is about the Irish and their drinking problems: "Catholicism and whiskey are the staples of life," the woman is saying. My curiosity is killing me, so finally I turn my head to see what they look like; she has red hair.

I even like imagining *this* couple's life—are they romantically involved or just friends? On this particular day, I like to think they're together.

He's just asked for the check, and I feel a little anxious and a little sad. I want to go with them in some way.

As he stands up to pay, he asks if she wants to walk him home; he has to get a shower before work.

I hear the waitress speaking to the two girls at the table in front of me: "Who gets the pancakes?" In her other hand she holds a large salad.

By this time the red-haired woman has stood up and the breeze blows her summer skirt like in a movie.

I don't know why, but right now I already miss this man with his shower and job to go to; I miss the woman with her out-of-season skirt and the girl who got the pancakes.

Lulu called today. She wants to come visit. I told her any sister of mine is welcome anytime. She has never been to New York, and I told her I could show her a thing or two (or three or four). It seems that life in Indiana after a divorce is no better than life in Indiana during a bad marriage. It's too bad, really; she was so sure that things were going to go her way once she was an independent woman again. She talked my ear off about what a nineties sort of life she was going to be living once everything was cleared up.

Losing her job slowed down her plans, though, and when her dog was stolen, she felt as if fate was, for some reason, against her knowing any kind of happiness. Not that the dog meant anything to her—she had found him in the first place. It was the thought that if she had been home, then things could have been very dire indeed. For two days after the first ransom note arrived, all she could say to anyone was, "Damn, that dog could've been me."

Somehow talking to Lulu always helps me put all of my problems into perspective. My life might be out of whack, but hers is certifiably insane.

She said she was planning to come visit in October because that would give her enough time to have a few garage sales to raise a little extra spending money. If she ever does make it here, she'll probably want to stay. I can't imagine she would have much to go back to after three garage sales.

Mom has taken this move of mine a little too personally. She finally called me tonight after not speaking to me since I've been here. The first thing I'd done when I got to New York was call home—even before unloading the car.

"Guess where I am," I said.

She couldn't, not in a million years.

Tonight, she asked why I couldn't have at least told them when I was home at Christmas what I was planning to do. I guess she doesn't realize I didn't *plan* anything.

After she told me it's my life and that she and Dad only want me to be happy, she reminded me that I still have to eat and pay the rent. Thanks, Mom.

Apparently, even Jeannie was shocked—not the correct response from a Bohemian younger sister who's moved a dozen times all over the world—so I didn't tell her that I thought of her as I left my old life because it seemed like something *she'd* do.

I guess there's a big difference between never putting yourself in the real world in the first place and walking out on it. It's not like I chose to be born the responsible one.

Right now, I sort of feel like I did when I was twelve, when we drove to California for a vacation. I had a big road atlas in the backseat and I was memorizing the state capitals, when Dad started asking me for directions. I didn't mind; in fact, it was kind of an honor—that was until we ended up in a bad section of St. Louis, on the wrong side of the Missis-sippi.

That's not what caused the problem.

After I navigated us back to the interstate, I very deliberately let the atlas fly out the window. The sight of that book, crazily flapping away from us on four lanes of endless asphalt, reminded me that I'd never asked for the responsibility in the first place.

I had planned to do laundry after work today. Joe called as I was leaving, so I asked him to meet me there, glad that I would have someone to talk to. I got my stuff together and was at the Laundromat when I said I would be. Joe, on the other hand, wasn't, and a phone call to him thirty minutes later had him explaining that he had changed his mind.

"Thanks for letting me know," I said as I hung up the phone.

I know doing laundry is not a night on the town, but I really was looking forward to hanging out with Joe away from a bar and a pounding disco beat. I began to get very angry, swearing to myself that this was it, and that Joe and I were through. I shoved all my clothes into one washer and sat on a graffiti-covered plastic chair, prepared for the next two hours to be the longest I had ever known.

As my clothes were entering the spin cycle, a woman next to me whom I hadn't noticed before said, "That damn spin cycle is the hardest one to sit through. You just gotta sit and wait, and you know, it seems like forever."

I smiled and agreed with her, and we began to talk. She had three bags of groceries with her, and out of one she pulled a six-pack of Budweiser and offered me one. I gladly accepted and asked her name.

"Evelyn," she said as she cracked open her tall-boy.

Evelyn, I found out, made her living from selling pot on the corner of First and 10th. She has been dealing for thirteen years and would like to get out of the business, but "there ain't a whole lotta options for Hispanic girls who didn't finish high school." She laughed when she said this, but I didn't really believe that she thought it was all so funny. I told her about my situation with Joe, and she said that she, too, was having trouble with her love life. ("If somebody ain't where they s'posed to be when they s'posed to be, what's the point?")

I have to admit that I was feeling very close to Evelyn as I sipped my third beer. She told me that no matter what happens, she always sets aside time to do her laundry.

"Clean clothes say a lot," I said.

Evelyn agreed: "Ain't nobody gonna see me in no dirty-ass clothes on the corner. I got some pride."

Our laundry had long been folded and the beer long gone, when we decided it was time to go. I walked Evelyn up to the corner and told her I hoped to see her again.

"Just look for me on the street," she said. "You ain't gotta buy nothing."

"I will," I said as I headed off.

Walking home, I felt lucky to have met Evelyn. When I got in, I forgot I was mad at Joe, so I called him to tell him about her. And you know, all he could say was, "You're drunk."

"Yeah, well," I said, "at least my clothes are clean."

And once again, I hung up without saying good-bye.

I think I've finally found the perfect restaurant. When I saw the HELP WANTED sign in the window and walked in, I thought maybe it was closed because there was nothing going on, and there were no customers. A waitress was sitting at the counter with the Sunday *Times* spread out in front of her, and the bartender and busboy were tossing a lemon across the length of the restaurant.

The waitress, Jillian, quickly assured me they were open and this was the regular day shift. When I asked how they made any money, she said, "We don't, but you get all the enchiladas you can eat."

The bartender, Nick, said, "Don't scare her away. We get a whole half-hour rush at noon. And anyway, we're usually too hungover to handle any more than that."

They buzzed Tommy, the owner's son, to let him know I was inquiring about the job, and a few minutes later, this very young guy with wild hair and nervous laughter appeared. He didn't even ask me about my restaurant experience; as soon as he learned I had been in advertising, he broke into a passionate speech about an idea he has for a deodorant commercial.

I start tomorrow. No trailing necessary.

As I was getting my schedule, one of the night waiters came in, very good looking.

"J.C.," Jillian whispered to me as he walked by. "Gay."

Right before I left, the whole staff sat together at a table, where Tommy attempted to deliver a sort of lecture, amidst apologies.

"Geez, guys," he said. "You know how I hate to do this, but

I've got to crack down. No more staying until four A.M. The restaurant closes at eleven. You can have one margarita afterwards, but that's it."

I think this place just might work out.

Lunacy rules! Tonight at work I was not only called a cock-sucker, but a misogynist too! I have always been one to speak my mind and I encourage everyone to do so, but this was an attack I hadn't expected and was not at all prepared for.

I was doing my thing when out of nowhere this woman started saying that I was ignoring her and that I had been rude. I feigned remorse, but that didn't stop her. This thing kept building and building until I finally took her food from her, threw it in the bus tub and told her to get out.

That's where the misogyny accusations came in. It was a real scene. She started screaming, I was trying not to, and everyone else in the place was just staring. Finally she left, declaring like MacArthur, "I shall return." And she did. She opened the door twice after that to hurl some more hateful remarks my way. I kept thinking to myself, "I'm just a waiter. Do I really deserve this?"

Needless to say, any chance I had to make it to the end of the night in a decent frame of mind was shot. I spent the rest of my shift wondering why people are so twisted (myself included), and what the whole point of even trying is all about.

I've come to the conclusion that we try because we have no choice—or that the choices we do have are limited. (It's either life or death, baby.) I go on putting up a brave front, being a waiter and taking abuse because I know that when I die, then there will be peace.

Anyway . . . if there isn't peace when I die, at least I won't be waiting tables. That is, if I don't go to hell.

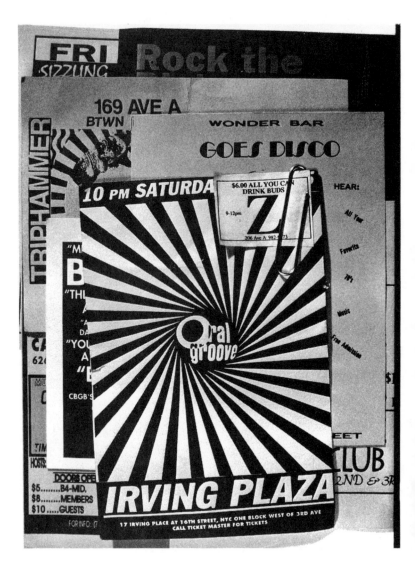

Last night after our shift drinks, Jillian suggested we all go out together. It was already the middle of the night, the time most people are already *home* from going out, but no one else seemed to notice.

Ever since I started this job, I can't seem to get right to sleep anymore. I go home after most shifts and stay up reading. I was secretly thrilled with this all-going-out idea. Outwardly, I acted as casual as anyone, like it was the most normal thing in the world to do at two A.M.

We went to this really dark, really small club called Z on A. It was nothing like those horrible pick-up places I'd been to in Ohio with people after work. Everyone in this place looked like they'd just shown up in the clothes they'd been wearing all day—black outfits that seemed shrugged on.

People were kind of swaying on the dance floor by them- selves with languid ghostlike movements. How else *could* you dance to Morrissey? I asked myself. That's the kind of music they played there. I don't think I've ever danced to music that I actually liked before. This was all different.

Out on the dance floor, faces melted. I'd catch a glimpse of J.C. or Jillian or Nick as they bobbed around, but it was like it was the first time I'd ever seen them. I found myself looking back at strangers for some secret recognition that I suddenly craved.

I saw a guy with long dark hair who looked a lot like Bono, dancing in the corner near me. Though his feet never left the ground, he seemed to be constantly rising above everyone else. The entirety of his dance seemed to be beckoning some- one or something beyond the room. There didn't seem to be anything left to connect him to anyone there.

Jillian was suddenly next to me. She nudged me and raised one eyebrow.

"Hot, huh?" she said, nodding toward the Bono-man and smiling in approval.

I shrugged and turned away from her. Why couldn't she see what I saw?

He wasn't about all of that pick-up stuff—of this I was certain as I saw him standing alone at the bar, talking and laughing with the bartender. His eyes would occasionally drift over the heads of the dancers, groping for something beyond, but definitely not a pick-up.

I suddenly wanted to be where his eyes went.

My second choice was the dance floor, which I didn't so much move to as let myself be pulled to by some unknown factor. Soon I found him next to me, dancing his solitary dance.

Then his reaching gaze suddenly settled itself on my face, and I felt my insides being pulled out toward it.

It was all too much; how could I begin to answer that enormous question in front of me?

So I tore my eyes away from it. I suddenly concerned myself with locating J.C., forming an ugly social smile as I waved a silly wave toward my friends across the room.

He wasn't there anymore when I focused again on the adjacent dancers. I searched every corner of the room, but he was gone, and all I wanted was for him to be there again, always.

I walked out into the strange blue light of dawn, a sliver of a moon hanging low in the sky. Birds were chirping and garbage trucks rattled to a stop every few feet. I imagined the words that he might have spoken clearly in my head: "It's faces that are beautiful. Faces and space and light and time." I just knew that he was a sculptor or a painter named Dominic or Malcolm and that he loved the dark black of wrought-iron fire escapes against the sun-washed redbrick buildings.

I felt him looking into my eyes again, only this time I looked back.

There is a God! At least tonight there was.

　　We did shots while closing up at work and before I knew it, I was loose on the streets in all of my just-buzzed-enough glory. I was feeling decidedly Southern, my mood no doubt influenced by the sweet breeze which was blowing New York's trash around at my feet and messing with the hair on top of my head. The moon was crescent and my mood was pleasant. I was ready to go.

　　I was headed east trying to figure out how I could get to New Orleans on the sixty-five bucks I had just made, when some guy handed me a flyer advertising a bar on Avenue A that was having a "Six bucks gets you all the beer you can swallow" night.

　　"Well, it ain't the French Quarter," I told myself in my best Cajun accent, "but it is cheap. And God knows I'd go to an execution at least once if there was a beer-blast going on."

　　I found the place (which was a delightfully dark hole in the wall), laid down my six singles, and headed for the beer. Except for the occasional solo spin on the dance floor, I spent the night holding up the bar, flirting with the bartender, and watching the crowd (who all looked like friends Sid and Nancy had left behind) doing their thing. I drank and stood and stared and drank some more before I was beckoned back outside by the stars in the sky. I walked home, singing all the way, and didn't see a soul I knew on the streets. Yessir, tonight was as close to heaven as this boy's been in a while.

　　"Jambalaya crawfish pie on the bayou."

Some amazing thought is still wisping around inside of me. It was crystal-clear in the bathroom in the middle of the night, but that was hours and dreams ago. Its essence is still inside of me.

How fleeting the best thoughts can be. They're like dreams you try to remember in the morning. I can still picture fragments of last night's dreams—flying rapidly over the city sidewalks, belly-down, almost skimming the ground; then, in a dream-flash, rocketing above the buildings where I caught a glimpse of that dreamy-eyed guy from Z. In a final dream non sequitur, I was caught in a shower of strawberries, grinning like a mad-woman.

I woke up doing the same. Which reminds me of that middle-of-the-night thought: I think it started to answer the question of the meaning of life. It feels like it.

My head seems to be unstoppable when it comes to forming ideas which to me are brilliant but to the rest of the world (I'm afraid) may seem only slightly interesting.

One never knows, though, when one's thoughts might be considered genius by another, so I've decided to record these ideas of mine in the hopes that one day I might be recognized by this world that so far has been ignoring me.

Idea #1—Aim Toothpaste

This little gem has been rattling around in my head for years. It involves a series of commercials which revolve around the slogan "I Aim to keep it that way," or "We Aim to keep it that way" if the spot involves a family. Of course, the shots would be of fresh-faced men and women and their kids, just home from a trip to the dentist where they all just received rave reviews. This brings them to my slogan, "We Aim to keep it that way," which they say proudly, displaying their pearly whites.

Note: Crest also a possibility. Song: *"Crest, Crest puts cavity worries to rest,"* etc. etc. etc.

Tonight at work I seated this tall, freckled regular whom I've noticed before, mainly because he bears the same kind of resemblance to Howdy Doody that Richie Cunningham always did. I even remembered that he always orders a Coke without ice and that the gray-haired gentleman who joins him later gets a margarita, straight up, with no salt.

I was gloating a little (like when a tourist picks *you* out of the crowd to ask for directions), confident that I was well on my way to becoming a real New Yorker. I had to let J.C. in on my latest development, considering that he always treats me like I'm walking around New York with a big neon "Ohio" sign printed across my forehead.

"See that regular over there?" I motioned, savoring the word "regular." "I just brought him a big old Coke, *no ice,* and I've already ordered his father's *straight-up* margarita." "His *father*?!" J.C. nearly shrieked. "Hey, Jilly! Come here, you've got to hear this one!"

The two of them were nearly in convulsions over my mistaken identification. After I confessed that I sometimes have a hard time figuring out which guys are gay, J.C. decided I needed to be educated.

After our shift, we jumped in a cab to head for J.C.'s favorite haunt.

"We are going *all out,*" he said, as the cab pulled up to the Roxy.

In one huge disco floor after another, gorgeous men were everywhere. There were also a few women dressed in sparkly black spandex; they flung their long hair around as they danced, in the same way I'd noticed Jillian dancing at Z. A strong disco beat was pumping, like straight out of *Saturday*

Night Fever. Then I saw "John Travolta," dancing up on a six-foot-high block. This guy was really *good*—he had the hair, the suit, the moves so exactly right that I almost wondered if . . . His face, it turns out, was as young as the real Travolta's would have been back when he was Vinnie Barbarino.

On another giant block, a guy half-dressed as Marilyn Monroe gyrated wildly. He was wearing a wig and makeup and the remains of a glittery dress, but he'd ripped the top of it off, so his naked male torso contrasted strangely with the platinum wig and eyelashes.

It was like a circus. On the other side of the room, a guy dressed in strips of leather shook the bars of what looked like a huge birdcage, which was placed over him.

I couldn't keep from staring out of pure fascination. I don't think I've ever seen anyone go to so much trouble to be willingly gawked at. It was all sort of noble, in a strange way.

When my eyes wandered to the next block, I must have gasped out loud because there was J.C., in nothing but his apron from work, playing the part of a *Flashdance* fantasy. I was just too embarrassed to watch him. Jillian appeared out of nowhere, just in time to see me turn away.

"Oh, come on," she teased. "Now's your chance to see what his ass looks like."

I mumbled something about needing to find the bathroom and pushed my way through some big swinging doors. In a ladies' lounge nicer than any I'd ever seen before were a dozen very *GQ*-looking men.

"Oh, I'm sorry," I murmured. "Wrong room."

"No, no, you're all right," a guy assured me, wiping his nose with a pressed handkerchief. "Go on in."

I glanced around quickly, hearing nothing but pleasant chatter in a roomful of people who all seemed to have colds. For a second, I thought I saw the guy from Z—the one who danced beyond everything in the room—but there was no way I thought that *he* would be in this place. This place is about being "on" and being seen, about enhancing life artificially; and *he's* only about being real. Of this I am certain.

In high school, Sister Edith told us all that drugs were bad news. I knew very little about drugs at that point, but I did know that it seemed like Sister Edith herself might be a bit of trouble. She did, after all, throw a human brain wrapped in cellophane at Ritchie Barrett's head. That episode alone was enough for me to question whether or not Sister was indeed doing the work of the Lord.

On the day she told us about the pain and despair that using drugs would bring into our lives, Sister Edith seemed more riled up than usual. I remember wondering how she could know so much about illegal substances. I had a little daydream in which Sister was a junkie. There she was, running down an alley from the cops and to escape, she jumped, habit and all, into a garbage Dumpster. When I started laughing in class, of course Sister used me as a target.

"What do you find so funny about this subject, laughing boy?" she asked.

"Nothing," I said, imagining she had a needle and some smack strapped to her leg under her outfit.

I caught her saying things like "evil" and "the devil" and "people who do that stuff end up hanging around outside of Woolworth's."

"You don't want to hang around in front of Woolworth's, do you?" she asked me.

"No, Sister," I answered, keeping it a secret that sometimes after school I would get on the bus and go downtown by myself just to watch those people in front of Woolworth's. They intrigued me with their wild eyes and paper bags covering up whatever it was they were drinking.

When the bell rang, Sister asked me to step up front. She sort of squinted her eyes into mine.

"You haven't gotten involved, have you?" she asked.

"No, Sister," I replied.

The rest of the year, she would every so often pull me aside in the hall and poke at my eyes with her stubby, holy fingers, looking for incriminating clues. She never found any, though. It wasn't until years later that I actually showed signs that I might belong in front of Woolworth's. I shudder to think of Sister Edith checking me today. I'm sure she comes equipped with a Breathalyzer and a blood kit by now.

This customer came into the restaurant today, sat at the bar, meekly ordered a club soda, and looked at me.

"Do you know why they invented video?" he asked.

I had no idea if this was the setup for a joke, if he was starting a sincere conversation, or if he suddenly had an urgent burst of curiosity about the origins of video.

"Nooo . . ." I answered, equally ambiguous.

"It was so that when they shot pornography it would be more exciting—more immediate. You know, you'd feel like you were really there."

I just stared at him. Had he said this with the slightest inflection of innuendo I would have had no doubt about his perversity. But he sounded like he had just read it out of *Encyclopedia Britannica* or something.

I sort of stared back at him with that strange half-smile that takes over your face when you can't think of anything to say. It was the second time today that something like this had happened to me.

Nick, the actor/bartender, came in earlier with a story about pornography, too.

Last night, he and his current girlfriend, Doreen, spent the evening apartment-sitting at her boss's apartment, taking care of the cats while her boss was out of town. Apartment-sitting is the New York, grown-up version of playing house. Before she even opened the first can of cat food, Nick was over. This overpriced cubicle became the equivalent of a honeymoon suite for them, since they both have roommates and seldom have a place to be alone.

Nick said they immediately got naked and lit every candle in the place. All in preparation for the video Nick was so looking forward to watching. (Boss's VCRs are an added luxury to the whole apartment-sitting game.)

Nick's memory of the porn movie seemed a lot more vivid than what actually took place with him and Doreen, but apparently his objective had been to duplicate the action on the screen. As he spoke, his eyes took on that glazed look that made me feel sorry for Doreen, a woman I don't even know. I wonder if he even realized what the real-life source of his pleasure looked like.

Anyway, at some point in this hot and heavy evening, Nick and Doreen became conscious of a strange odor, separate and distinct from their own activity. They stopped long enough to realize that the older (and half-blind) cat had leapt up on the shelf of candles and was now on fire.

Doreen was practically in hysterics, rolling the cat on the carpet and wondering how she was going to get rid of the singed section of fur so her boss wouldn't find out what had happened. Nick, meanwhile, was rewinding the part of the video they'd missed in the excitement—"the best part," he said.

Everyone in the restaurant howled at Nick's story—except me, with my stupid glued-on smile. J.C. said I was uptight.

I don't know, maybe.

I just remember once being mesmerized by a deepness in the eyes of a boy I liked because of what was there, in that deepness.

I remember how he pulled out these magazines one night and said he wanted to show me a few things.

I pretended to look for a while, feigning enthusiasm, feigning coolness, acting like I'd done this a million times before.

When stuff started happening between the two of us, I didn't stop him, because I remembered how I'd *wanted* it to happen so many nights when I was alone in my bed, in the moments right before I went to sleep.

When I looked for that deepness I loved in his eyes, they were stuck to some picture of a woman who wasn't even there.

Maybe J.C.'s right and I am uptight. Maybe I got away so fast that night because I didn't want to compete with some fantasy image on a page; but that's not the real reason I left.

I left because his eyes were dimmed with a glaze so thick I knew it had to be filling the holes where the deepness used to be.

I decided because of my mother-of-a-hangover not to go to work today. I instead chose to wander the streets in search of salvation. I was fairly certain that I wouldn't find it in Times Square, but I was horny, and you never know what surprises you might find in one of those bookstores. There have been plenty of times in my life when I was sure that all I needed to make things right was a stranger with a big dick.

It felt good to be outside. There was a slight breeze and it felt soothing against my skin. It seemed as if the wind was blowing all the ache right out of my head. I tried to think as little as possible, and I found that incredibly easy to do. Except for the occasional pre-anonymous-sex jitters, I was basically pleased with my seemingly stable frame of mind. I made it to Times Square surprisingly fast—I chose my pleasure venue and was in a booth with my fly open in what I believe was record time. No sooner had I gotten excited by the film I had selected when there was a rap on the door. Without missing a beat, I opened the door ever so slightly and left it ajar, like all professional public display artists know how to do.

At first I couldn't see anyone, but then a semi-attractive blond guy walked by, casting his eyes in the direction of my love cubicle. Now, it is customary to cruise for, I would say, about two to three minutes before entering a stranger's booth to mess around. And these few minutes of waiting I have no problem with. Well, it must have been at least ten minutes, and this guy must have walked by the door about a hundred times before the strangest thing happened: I suddenly realized what I was doing.

There I was in that dark little space with my pants down, playing with myself. I had my dick in my hand and I was waiting for some timid stranger to gather up the courage to come in and touch me. I suddenly felt ill; and this was no hangover.

Joe came crashing in on my mind. I have someone in my life who wants to love me and loves to have sex with me. What's the deal here? What am I doing?

I was out of that booth and onto Eighth Avenue in seconds. I felt mad. Why hadn't I gone to work?! I attacked myself with questions for the rest of the day and could give myself no answers. I can't understand this change in me. Where is the guy who felt no guilt and cared only about himself? I don't like being aware, goddammit. What good are questions that have no answers? What good are answers that go against everything you ever thought you felt? Needless to say, I've spent the rest of today feeling sad and stupid. I haven't answered the phone once, and Joe has left three messages.

It's funny—I remember when sex used to turn me on. Now it seems to turn me inside out.

It's been a double-shift, no-sleep, most-pounding-headache-imaginable kind of a day, but I feel surprisingly elated. All day long I dragged through my waitress chores in a fog, alternating between nausea and slap-happiness. My mind was in that automatic-pilot mode which makes even wiping dirty Plexiglas tabletops numbly pleasant. Customers' whiny little requests sounded like nothing more than white noise.

We all went to Z again last night after our shift drinks. I'd already emptied half the bottle of Jagermeister in the restaurant and was a little concerned that Tommy might get suspicious, but Nick assured me he'd only be ecstatic that his new bar product was so popular.

We left the restaurant late as usual, and skipped down Avenue A. I'm convinced that night air truly is different than air in the day—it's as if when the light leaves the sky, the space it had occupied becomes filled with an invigorating sort of alternative energy. Anyway (I reasoned out loud), if I felt this good to begin with, who knew how amazing the night could end up? Jillian said I was just buzzed beyond belief.

The doorman at the club remembered us from last time.

"No more slam-dancing to Lulu," he said, displaying emotion you wouldn't expect to find in a Hell's Angel his size. "'To Sir with Love' is a beautiful song."

We agreed—we were the ones who had requested it.

As soon as we got inside, Jillian underwent her usual transformation—it was as if she had just slid on a pair of ultra-cool shades in a room far too dark to need them. I found it a little unnerving, but every guy in the vicinity responded by looking at her like they just *had* to try on those glasses of hers. And all this without the actual existence of any form of eyewear.

A very medium looking guy headed toward us. I vaguely remembered Jillian talking to him last time.

"Oh, no," Jillian said to me under her breath. "Cling-on."

"Hi, Holly!" he said to Jillian, far too brightly.

I'd heard Jillian give this name, among others, in answer to the always-predictable pick-up line. But it was a mystery to me how she could stand there and carry on such an animated conversation with him, leaning in closely at times, when she'd later complain to me that she couldn't get rid of him. Of course, I probably could have learned something from her. I mean, no one, not even a cling-on, was talking to me.

I could have dissolved into a self-pitying mess at this point, but then I noticed *him* again, the Z-man himself, leaning against his favorite spot at the bar, smiling a little to himself. The bartender was handing him a beer and they were clinking bottles in their casual toast way. I sensed that he talked to people because he wanted to, not because he was looking to get something from them.

After he took a long swig of his beer, he set it on the bar and walked out to the dance floor and started dancing. Even though I loved the song and wanted to dance too, I was feeling the slightly catatonic side effects of my earlier medicinal beverage intake, so I had to be content to watch.

How could he be so *alone* in a roomful of people, so oblivious to all around him? His world seemed so clearly preferable to the one the rest of us were stuck in that I felt ashamed of my earlier impulse to try to fit into it. Then his dancing image melted in my mind into a series of montagelike pictures—it was as if I was seeing his whole life flash before my eyes: him, the sculptor, dusted in white powder, frowning in concentration at the beautiful form he'd just created; him, running alongside his big faithful dog in Tompkins Square Park; him, walking alone down St. Marks Place like it was a long, empty highway . . . right into the sunset. I saw him talking earnestly over coffee about all of the soul-searching questions he'd faced so far, and all the dreams he had yet to see.

His favorite books: anything by Salinger, *Anna Karenina,* and *The Great Gatsby.*

His favorite music: seventies and rock.

His sign: Taurus.

His . . . (I was obviously lost in my dreamscape.)

Just then, I saw Jillian in a corner with her "shades" back on, nervously smoking and motioning to me. I reluctantly pulled myself away from my thoughts of him and walked over to her table.

"This scene is so old already," she complained. "Now I have to *hide* all night."

"It's okay with me," I said, settling into the shadows where I could openly stare at him again.

"What are you waiting for?" Jillian asked, after noticing my fixed gaze.

I shrugged. What was I supposed to do—go up with a cling-on line and ask him his name?

"He doesn't exactly seem like the type who makes the first move," she said.

"Oh, he moves," I answered knowingly.

"Well, if you don't jump on it soon, you're gonna miss the ride."

I doubted it. He simply wasn't like that. I knew it.

I can hear him now, as he'd sound talking to me over coffee:

"The big jump," he'd say, "is to not just live *your* life, but to live Life."

See?

For some reason, it feels like a holiday out tonight. The streets are wet, shiny with light, and empty. It's a night made for feeling melancholy, which isn't an altogether bad way to feel, in my book. In fact, I've always thought it kind of a comforting feeling, in a weird way. When you're just sad enough to notice things like people waiting alone at bus stops or couples eating in diner windows, things like that are good to notice. Stuff that helps you say, "See, I ain't the only one."

I went to my favorite new watering hole after work. When I first got there, the place was empty except for a guy at the pinball machine and two girls on the dance floor. I got a beer, found my usual spot at the bar, and leaned. Sly Stone was singing, *I am everyday people,* as the girls on the dance floor carried on like it was the best tune either of them had ever heard. Watching them was a kick. These two girls were having a fucking riot out there, jumping and spinning around under a couple of dinky lights like it was Studio 54 or something.

Every time the chorus would come along, they would get extra excited, throw their arms up in the air and look right into each other's eyes, bobbing their heads and mouthing the words, their smiles so huge it looked like they had the moon in their mouths. *I am everyday people,* they would sing, and they were, too. They looked so ordinary, so perfectly everyday that I wanted to run out onto the dance floor and say, "Hey! Are you guys from Indiana? You look like you could be. I am. How long have you been in New York?"

I would have, too, but just as I was about to slide out there, the song was over and they were gone, leaving the floor empty except for a billion specks of light reflecting off the tiny disco ball hanging in the middle of the room.

I woke up feeling kind of sick and utterly unable to sleep, so after pulling on some clothes, I sat out on the cool, cement doorstep to the roof and contemplated the summer to come. What do the poor souls without roof access do?

For all my bragging about relishing a "real" city summer without an air conditioner, I was already sweating and irritable, and it was only the second of June. Yet in some strange way, this was precisely what I meant when I thought of a real summer in New York.

I heard the *click* of someone's air-conditioning going on (wimps!) and felt superior in my own lack-of-air-conditioner-ness. Not that I wouldn't spend the summer running eagerly from one air-conditioned haven to the next, but I didn't really *need* one—not for what I was supposed to experience.

No, better to wake up to the cool, blue five-o'clock dawn and sit on the chilled cement roof stoop. I very nearly fell back asleep sitting there thinking.

It's seven-thirty and once again, here I am leaning against Tower Records, Joe's fricking home away from home. He's buying yet another Barbra Joan Streisand CD.

This has got to stop—me waiting for Joe, Joe waiting for me. It's a game that I've grown tired of. And now, on top of his insane preoccupation with all things Streisand, he's been getting on me about my drinking, the little bastard. It was drinking that brought us together in the first place. In fact, I think it's the only thing we've ever had in common, and now he wants me to put the bottle down and reevaluate our situation.

Fine, I'm all for change. But does it have to involve AA?

I ran into *him* today coming out of Tower Records. The guy from the Z club. We were both wearing our Walkmans. I was listening to that early Aztec Camera tape—the one that Liza in San Francisco taped for me. I was just thinking how that was about the time things really started changing for me—when I found out there was an undercurrent in the world that I never knew existed. This current consisted of everything inside of me that had never fit in anywhere before. I mean, whoever heard of Aztec Camera? Yet their lyrics seemed to come from *my* soul and carried across even the abyss I had placed between myself and the world.

So there I was, caught inside myself, when *he* walks out of the revolving door at Tower. We both stopped a little as we caught sight of each other, stared (as per usual), and went through that time-frozen hesitation in which you know *some-thing* has to happen. (But of course, didn't.)

In shyness I immediately looked away—down at my Walk-man, where I became suddenly quite absorbed in adjusting the volume or something. Something meaning nothing. When I looked up again, he was gone.

Now I'm dying inside. I know what *should* have (what I would have loved to have) happened—the unreal reality is safe in my head:

I'd be fumbling around with my Walkman controls and suddenly there'd be a shadow across my hands, and these beautiful fingers would brush across mine to shut off the tape. I'd look up, and he'd be inches from my face, staring at me. He'd gently open the Walkman and pull out the tape to look at it. He'd smile slowly, put the tape back in, and push the Rewind button.

While the tape was rewinding, he'd open his little yellow Tower Records bag and pull out the store-bought version of the same tape. I'd knowingly smile as he put it in his Walkman.

"Ready?" he'd say softly.

"Of course," I'd easily reply.

We'd position our index fingers over our respective Play buttons, and he'd begin: "One, two, three—"

Click.

The virtuous music would begin and we'd start walking—in our own worlds but definitely together—and, like two happy idiots, we'd sing along with the simultaneous broadcast of our tapes: *"I hear your footsteps in the street, won't be long before we meet, it's obvious . . ."*

Sitting on the subway today I thought of how brave we all are. Fighting to get close despite how much we know. It is no secret that love is both simple and arduous and usually short-lived. It is indeed a fact that when people want to love so badly that it becomes their aim in life they will only come up empty.

Love cannot be put on a list of things to do; it cannot be blueprinted.

(Ignorant Genius)

I prayed tonight at the club—on the dance floor while the lights were flashing and the percussion was shaking my heart. I looked around and thought, if everybody else knew what I was doing, they'd probably think I was crazy; they'd probably also assume that *God* would think I was crazy too. But that didn't keep me from asking for a teeny little celestial favor—to be able to speak to *him* tonight.

Later, I found him dancing next to me, more intensely than ever, and when the song was over we stopped face-to-face. My mouth was open.

"Excuse me," I finally said. But the voice I heard wasn't mine; I had spoken with a very pronounced English accent. Where had that come from? Not since the days when Jeannie and I used to play Cockney Girls, screeching at each other in atrocious accents, had such a sound come out of my mouth.

"Yes?" he said politely.

"Sorry," I said, hoping the accent continued to hold up. "But do you think you might tell me your name?"

Before he could say another thing, I rushed on, shrilling a bit in true Cockney Girl form.

"You see, it's simply a game I play, guessing Americans' names."

Before he could answer, I ran away and hid in the bath-room, embarrassed beyond belief. I re-lived the whole incident in my head, where my prayer was answered in another way:

I'd be standing at the bar, still embarrassed by my earlier blunder. From behind me, I'd hear a guy order a Heineken. A guy with a strong German accent.

"Ja voy," he'd say. *"Prost!"*

Something about his corny, overearnest tone would make me turn around to glance at him.

There *he* would be, with a silly grin on his face, holding a beer stein in the air.

"I give you challenge in your game," he'd say in that ridiculous accent. "My name is Johann. You never guess *that,* no?"

Then the Johann imposter would kiss the Cockney Girl imitator, and neither would remember anymore *what* language they spoke, who they were, or where they came from.

This morning I woke up at the usual far-too-early time to ready myself for my day. After I took my shower, I was getting dressed when I happened to glance over at Joe, who was sleeping in my bed. Now I know we broke up, but last night involved excessive drinking, and we decided at some point that there are plenty of friends who sleep together and avoid all of the other trappings of a relationship. Such as what, I can no longer remember. All I know is that we had sex, and any progress we had made to become friends is now out the window. Still, Joe did look beautiful lying there. I had a tiny little daydream in which he starred, but I quickly got myself together and reminded myself how much he bugs me, gave him a kiss on his bare ass, and left him sleeping in my apartment.

I made good time to the subway, and the train came right away, which is always good (spending too much time underground makes me angry). When the train stopped at Spring Street, I got off like I always do, but there seemed to be at least a thousand more people than usual rushing toward the gates. And all the way down the platform, just beyond the gates, there was a big fat man with a tiny little mustache. He was wearing one of those beige trench coats, buttoned all the way up, and he had the coat's belt wrapped tightly around his waist. I could see he had something in his hand, which turned out to be one of those counting gadgets.

It seems someone had placed this trussed-up man in the subway with this archaic counting device and asked him to click it every time someone left through the gate. Now I'm not the head of any big company, and I never did much like math in school, but even I could tell you that with all those people stepping all over each other to get out of that hole, that man's records ain't going to be very accurate.

So anyway, I let the fat man note that I do indeed exist, and I walked up the stairs to the outside world. I crossed Lafayette and began walking toward work. When I reached Wooster, one of those annoying car alarms went off. This I've heard a million times, so I was all prepared to dismiss it as just another attack on my right to exist peacefully, when all of a sudden, I heard someone whistling. But not just a whistle whistle; someone whom I could not see was whistling the exact same tune as the goddamn car alarm!

While being tortured by this disturbing musical duet, I noticed a slightly opened door, and sort of just sticking out (or maybe just stuck), was this old woman's head. She wasn't doing anything as far as I could tell. As I walked by, her eyes widened and she gave me a big "Hey."

"Hey," I said back to this floating granny head while still being serenaded by the bodyless whistle in the background. Needless to say, my senses were overloading and I hadn't even gotten to work yet.

I was exhausted, man. I felt like I was going to be totally useless at work. And I was.

After work I got a phone call from a guy with a thick accent, who insisted he knew me. I kept telling him I didn't think so and was ready to hang up, but then he mentioned Isabelle. After I determined that he was actually talking about my sister, I stayed on the line.

Apparently, my sister Izzy had given him my number when she found out he was traveling to New York. She knew how much I'd always wanted to travel in Europe, so I guess she thought this was some kind of substitute.

I told him I'd meet him later for a drink at Downtown Beirut. I didn't want to take him to Z on the off chance that my guy might be there and think I was "with" someone. As soon as I hung up, I called home.

"Did I forget to tell you?" Izzy said. "Oops."

It turns out she met this guy Axel at the Raven, a new coffeehouse adjacent to the local youth hostel that I didn't even know existed. When *I* was in high school, the Ohio custom was to drive to empty parking lots for inane keggers; we never even met anyone from out of state, let alone Berlin.

When I walked into Downtown Beirut an hour later, it was practically empty so I grabbed the opportunity to play "Seasons in the Sun" on the jukebox without anyone glaring at me. A tall sallow guy with large sideburns and carrying a backpack walked in and headed straight for a corner.

I went over and asked if he was Axel, somehow feeling like a groupie by just uttering that name.

He grunted and nodded, then before I even sat down, said, "What is this shit?"

I guess my jukebox selection wasn't going to go unnoticed after all.

I sort of laughed and ordered a Jagermeister, to which he repeated, "What is this shit?" after trying it. I felt like it would have been bad host manners to point out that it came from his native country.

We got into somewhat of a conversation after Nirvana came on the jukebox and he started tapping his boot. Except everything we talked about seemed to bring out that same obsession with feces in him. I kept trying to convince myself this was a real live example of German black nihilism, but it sure didn't lend itself to inspiring conversation.

When I finally got up to leave, he stood up as well, shouldering his backpack. Something told me he thought he was coming with me.

It seems Izzy also forgot to mention that she told him she was sure it would be okay for him to stay with me since he was completely broke.

We went back to my apartment where his huge pack seemed to take up half the floor. I suddenly couldn't envision getting any sleep while he was sacked out five feet from me.

He must have felt the same way, because his hollow face actually came close to lighting up when I suggested we go out again. I took him to the Village Idiot, where it's so loud and obnoxious that I figured we wouldn't have to talk. Oddly enough, he found the country music fascinating.

The beautiful magic of alcohol finally kicked in, and his face began to seem almost friendly to me—especially after one of the more boisterous drunks punched me in the arm and said, "You two are so grim. Are you from England or something?" From then on, we were in it together.

The night progressed to a predawn tour of the Lower East

Side, and we found ourselves in the middle of the Brooklyn Bridge before we even realized we'd decided to cross it. A kid on a red bicycle was riding wildly toward us, but he paused long enough to snap a Polaroid of us and tossed it back as he rode off.

In the slowly-spreading dawn light, we strained to see the picture emerge from the darkness. Lights in the city were going off, and the sun was coming up, so we finally gave in and decided to go back to get some sleep. We never did see how the Polaroid turned out. We must have dropped it somewhere along the way.

When I was a kid, I heard that we humans use only ten percent of our brains' power. I think it was Walter Cronkite who told me. Actually, he didn't tell me personally. Every night at the same time his voice would come from the television in our family room, and in that gravelly, concerned tone he would spill the world's beans as I sat in the kitchen watching my mom mash potatoes and toss salads.

That night over dinner the talk was all about brains and whose was the biggest. I remember making Lulu spill her glass of milk and run from the table crying when I joked that hers was probably the size of a pea. For nights after I heard the news, I would lie in my bed and squint my eyes hard, trying to jump-start my jalopy of a brain. In the morning, I would follow Lulu and my mom around the house with a dictionary, hounding them to ask me to spell words I had never heard, in order to see if my mind-revving exercises worked.

This afternoon we had a waiters' meeting which nearly did in my shaky gray matter. The subject was water. We were introduced to a salesman from San Pellegrino who spent an hour and a half giving us tips on how to better sell his product. I'm all for the working man, but this guy's job seems sadly silly. It's the only water we sell. They will either buy it, or they won't.

His spiel ended with a tasting of the stuff. Tiny cups were filled and passed around the room. I took mine and said under my breath (or so I thought), "This is ridiculous."

"Did you have something to say?" the manager asked from behind me.

 "This is delicious," I said with a smile, tossing my Dixie cup into the trash.

 I am in grave danger of losing what few smarts I do have. For years I have blamed the demise of my brain cells on my excessive ways, but today the true reason was revealed to me. My mind for more than two decades has been exposed to the real enemy—everyday life. I can only hope that I have discovered this in time to invent a stupidity-filtering cap with which to prevent any further nonsense from penetrating my already black-and-blue brain.

Marci is dropping in for a visit.

Actually, she's been planning this trip since I moved here. It's kind of like the highlight of her year and I just sort of forgot about it.

It's not that I don't want to see her. We spent enough all-nighters together when we were in college to form a real bond, but lately, I have a hard time calling up any actual memory of those times. To me, it's more like watching an old home movie of someone else's life. Not bad, kind of familiar and interesting, but just not mine.

The last time I saw Marci was a year out of college. She had moved to Pittsburgh and was an entry-level pharmaceutical professional. At the same time, I had become an entry-level advertising exec. I think we even shopped for our interview suits together then.

Marci was at a convention back in Columbus then, and because of her tight schedule, she asked if I could meet her at the Hilton lobby between seminars. I went there straight from work and we stood in a taupe-and-mauve hallway that was car-peted all the way around, from floor to walls to ceiling. I think there must have been a drinking fountain or something nearby, because people kept passing between us as we talked.

I felt sadder than I should have at the amount of effort it took me to keep our conversation going. Then it hit me as we stood there: the last time I had been in an overly coordinated hotel lobby like that was when I first drove into Columbus to look for a job. I had used the burgundy-and-beige lobby of the Ramada then as my office, since I didn't have a base right in the city. It didn't seem the least bit strange to me to get all dressed up in suburbia, then drive downtown and head straight to the hotel. No one even noticed as I used their row of public phones to set up interviews, lounging on the formless plush chairs between appointments. I even had a story ready, a fake name and all, if anyone questioned me.

A year later, talking to Marci in another bustling lobby, I forgot the details of my fabulous and intricate lie. Instead, I realized that I would no longer dream of pulling off such a thing and—worse yet—didn't even have the need to anymore.

Idea #2—Children's Television

New directions in programming. Out with the old and in with the new. A series of cartoons with an intellectual twist:

1. "Boy Kafka"—children will instantly identify with Boy as he struggles to come to grips with life and all its unpredictabilities by way of a diary in which he jots down all his thoughts which are brought to life by the magic of animation.

2. The animated "On the Road"—children will delight in the very real adventures of Dean and Sal and their stories of travel, women, and alcohol. Each show will end with a Kerouac poem read by an aging character known as Johnny Beat.

3. "Those Little Rolling Stones"—a live-action series in which actors portray the rock stars as children, and we see just what could drive a child into the arms of rock 'n' roll fame.

The possibilities I'm coming up with are endless. I'm currently thinking through an idea for a show about the great political Kennedy family. Working title: "The Cartoon Kennedys."

Today was an unexpected joy.

Marci showed up at my place in a turquoise maternity sweatsuit and didn't flinch at my cubicle of an apartment. I was expecting horrible conversation gaps, but as we sipped our tea, words that I hadn't even realized I was holding inside poured out of me. I found myself telling her about the guy from Z.

"You know all *that* without even talking to him?" She sounded less incredulous than in awe.

"I just know, I can feel that he's different. I guess maybe my mind has filled in some details."

"It's got to be a better way of occupying your brain than doing storyboards for salad dressing," Marci said with a slow grin.

She'd just left her pharmaceutical career to become a full-time mother, much to everyone's chagrin. We realized with a conspiratorial laugh that we were now both drop-outs.

Marci wanted to go shopping for some cheap electronic toys for her husband, so I suggested we roam down Broadway.

We weren't getting any real shopping done, and the sky was darkening with an approaching storm, but we couldn't stop walking down that long strip of cement. It was as if those tall buildings had hypnotized us.

A couple of flashes of close lightning sent pedestrians rushing into stores, but I've never heard of lightning striking any-one in New York City. Lightning strikes farmers in small towns in Ohio or golfers at country clubs, there's just too much here in New York for lightning to single out any one person.

Marci didn't seem concerned with the lightning, either. We just grinned at each other and walked even faster, feeling like nothing could stop us. It didn't matter that we weren't really going anywhere. We seemed to be just going.

One moment the cement and stone all around us were darkening with rain, the next there was only a silvery yellow burst of brilliant energy. I could see outlines of things, but the things themselves had disappeared. There was a sound of thunder, I suppose, but even it was consumed by the light. By the time Marci and I looked at each other, our eyes and mouths gaping, it was gone. The yellow glow made Broadway shimmer, an aftereffect visible only to us.

People around us were watching us carefully, in awe or shock.

"I think we were supposed to be struck," Marci said.

"I think we *were* struck," I said.

Then we looked at each other and started laughing.

Later, Marci would insist it was the protective aura of her unborn child that surrounded us and kept us safe from harm. All I know is we lived for a moment in beautiful lightning, which never would have happened if we weren't exactly where we were supposed to be at that time.

I have been offered a new position. This guy named Randy who comes into the restaurant every now and then asked if I would like to cook for his catering company. Cooking has never interested me much, really, but as nothing truly interests me, I'm thinking maybe this wouldn't be any less interesting than everything else. My career at the restaurant has pretty much run its course (the manager, in fact, tells me that the next person who asks about a job gets mine), and I have been itching for, oh, about six months to get out.

I can fry an egg, I told this Randy guy. He said that was more than enough experience.

Hmm . . .

Izzy. She's at it again.

I got another phone call from some backpacking Euro-
peans—this time it was a couple of university students from
Poland. Greggor and Annka were already in the neighborhood
when they called, so they showed up on my doorstep a few
minutes later.

I felt a twinge of recognition when I looked into their wide,
open faces, I guess because my ancestors are from their sister
country.

When I was in grade school, we had to do our family trees
à la *Roots*. I'd been somewhat mortified that I came from a
country no one had ever heard of or could even pronounce.
Then when I was in college and impressed by the history of my
ancestors' country, I was surprised to learn that when my grandmother had lived there, the country I thought I was from didn't
even exist yet. And now, sort of full circle, it doesn't exist again.
No wonder I'm having an identity crisis.

It was a gray, drizzly day. My new blood siblings and I
walked around the Village anyway. I showed them some of the
beautiful old architecture around Washington Square Park, but
they didn't seem very impressed. Greggor pointed out that
there are buildings in his town that are over six hundred years
old—"like your Czechoslovakia." I felt a little cheated out of
something.

I found myself playing the part of the unwilling hero tonight at work. I was waiting on a table of women who were celebrating a friend's divorce, when all of a sudden, the blondest woman at the table started screaming, "Oh, look! Oh, gross! Oh, gawd!" I looked toward the door to see what could possibly be the cause for such an "oh"-filled statement and saw a very dirty, disheveled man standing in the doorway.

My first inclination was to seat him at the table next to the gay divorcees, but I instead took him by the arm and led him outside. He gave me some shit about touching him and said in a voice that sounded as tired as he looked, "Hey, man, what's your problem?"

"I'm sorry," I said, "but you can't go messing with people in the restaurant."

"I ain't messing with nobody, and how do you know I wasn't gonna eat something anyway?"

I felt like an asshole. How did I know? I couldn't come out with the truth—"Well, sir, by the looks of you, it's obvious that you don't have a dime, and it makes it a lot easier for those of us who do if you just stick to wandering around outside."

I turned and looked through the window. The blonde divorced woman was laughing with her head thrown back. I hated her.

I turned back to the guy and said, "Look, there's no problem. It's just that the place is full. What do you say you let me buy you a beer?"

We went across the street to the deli where I bought him a quart of beer and a pack of Camels. I then walked him to the corner bus stop where I left him on the bench. When I got back to the restaurant, the manager was pissed.

"What the fuck are you making friends for? Your shift's not over yet."

He did thank me for removing the "kook" but added, "Next time, just show him the sidewalk. You got work to do."

By this time, it was ten-thirty and all my tables were gone except for the single ladies. I asked if I could turn my table over to another waiter.

"He can keep the tips," I said as I got my coat.

"All right," the manager said, "but you stay till close the rest of the week."

Fine, I thought, and pushed my way out the door, accompanied by the laughter of drunken diners. Out on the street, I lit a cigarette and went to the deli to get a beer for the walk home. On my way back past the restaurant, I saw that the other waiter had begun to put chairs up around the table of women whom I had started to wait on, what seemed like hours before. I walked to the corner, but when I got to the bus stop, the man was gone. I looked around for a while, but there was no sign of him. I continued walking, and as I finished my beer, I found myself wishing I had stayed with him.

Right in the middle of the lunch rush today, Nick announced that he knows where U2 hangs out when they're in town. Nick's roommate, James, who works in a tanning salon, is apparently chummy with the owner of a new East Village restaurant. This tanned owner told him that Bono and the gang have been at his place for the last three nights, playing pool and casually min- gling with the neighborhood regulars. And *tonight,* Nick said, they would definitely be back, because they had made reser- vations for a dinner party.

It turns out this Café Tabac is right in the neighborhood. I tried to get Jillian to go along with me, but she said she's given up groupie tendencies. Before I even had a chance to ask him, J.C. quickly informed me, "I hate that band, and I hate that place." What a bundle of sunshine he is.

When ten o'clock rolled around (it seemed like the prime celebrity dining hour), I set out for Café Tabac by myself. I was dressed in hanging-out clothes that clearly stated "nothing spe- cial about tonight—I just feel like playing pool." Too bad when I got there, everyone else's ultra-chic outfits boasted, "We're the young and beautiful."

I kind of slunk up to the bar, trying to figure out where a pool table would be in a place like this. The café was so small you could see the whole sparkling room at one glance: pol- ished brass, polished wood, crystal glasses reflecting candle- light, diamond smiles reflecting ego-light, but no pool table—and no U2.

I left without even having a drink, not nearly as disap- pointed about the absence of U2 as by the presence in that place. Walking up the street toward me were Greggor and Annka, on their way back to my apartment. I told them about the alleged U2 dinner party, and the way their faces lit up, there was no way I couldn't try at least one more time to track down the band. Back we went.

Since we couldn't exactly go up to the bartender and ask where Bono was, I decided to inquire about the pool table. The bartender nodded toward some stairs in the back.

Standing guard was a skinny rock 'n' roll guy with a clipboard. (Just seeing a rocker with something as official as a clipboard is enough to stop anyone.) He asked if we were on the list.

Innocently, I said we just wanted to play pool, that we were supposed to meet our friend, James, upstairs—James, a friend of the *owner*.

The rocker reacted just as I do when people try to pull that crap with me: His face glazed over and he shook his head.

"Is the owner here?" I asked, pushing my bluff.

He looked a little nervous. "Somewhere."

Then I faltered, not because I was afraid to talk to some hot-shot artificially bronzed restaurateur, but because of how I was starting to treat this guy who was just doing his job.

I looked him straight in the eye and said, "Look. I've got these people from Poland here, and they just want to play pool. Can't you please just let us play pool?"

Greggor and Annka, who were standing a short distance behind me, perked up when they saw us looking at them. Their wonderful moon-faces broke into beaming smiles that no one could have denied.

"Okay," he said reluctantly, and let us up the stairs.

Annka wanted to run right into the dining room, but Greggor and I thought it would be more casual if we just played pool and waited for the band to join us. Alone in a glorious red pool room, we proceeded to get drunk waiting for U2.

The rocker with the clipboard finally came in the room and said we had to finish up—they were closing. We rushed to the doorway, and the entire second floor was now empty. We had missed them. I guess they really don't play pool, after all.

I went back to the pool table for my last shot, glancing up at Greggor and Annka. Those beaming smiles were back on their faces, directed toward the doorway behind me. Then they started waving. Sweetly waving, like how you wave to your grandmother. Waving like those mechanical dolls in "It's a Small World" at Disneyland.

I turned around, and there was Bono, leaning against the elegant door frame.

There was only one thing I could have possibly done, although when I'd always dreamed of this moment, I never came up with this particular scenario.

I waved to Bono too.

I've decided to take the new job. The life I've been living is no life for me anymore, and the more I think about getting out of here, the more I like the idea. I would have quit this hellhole a long time ago if I had an option, but going to yet another restaurant didn't seem like it would solve anything.

Now I have an opportunity to do something I've never wanted to do before.

The idea of learning something (anything) does seem like a semi-interesting concept. It is a bit peculiar, I admit, that a stranger, to whom I've admitted I have no diploma from Le Cordon Bleu in my past, has offered me a job cooking. One can only assume that it's not my chicken à la king recipe he's interested in. But on the other hand, I don't know him well enough to say that he's not on the up and up—besides, I have no choice. Chances are I'll end up on a manslaughter charge if I stick around here much longer, and though I've only been interested in swallowing food in the past, I'm sure I could learn to like dealing with it on a more personal level.

The truth is, I have to like it. This guy and his recipes are my ticket out of this dump. (I like that—it sounds like a line from a gay Jimmy Cagney movie.) If it so happens that he is interested in more than just my dishpan hands, I'll handle it just like I do everything else. I'll ignore him.

How does this keep happening (unless, as I hate to think for fear of jinxing it, it's Destiny)? I ran into *him* again today, on the Staten Island Ferry. I never take the Staten Island Ferry, but this morning I woke up restless and wanted to get away, to see water, to feel like I was going somewhere, and the ferry came to mind. I suppose it's possible he lives over there, but if he does, then why do I keep seeing him all over Alphabet City, at places like the drycleaner's?

No, he must have just wandered around today with the same obscure destination in mind as me.

He was standing at the back rail when I boarded; I glanced up (it would have been *my* place of choice to stand), and I think a pale smile of recognition crossed his face when our eyes met.

But I quickly looked away—what if he thought I was *following* him or something? I mean, he must realize I don't live on Staten Island either (and he may not believe in Destiny).

I made my way to a side rail where I strained unsuccessfully to see him. With the lower-Manhattan skyline as a backdrop and the sun sparkling everywhere around us, it would have been the perfect place for us to finally meet formally, you know.

A small, middle-aged woman stood beside me, her eyes closed against the strong breeze. She looked down and fumbled in her purse for something, then pulled out a pack of crumpled cigarettes. The cigarette she placed in her mouth was curved ludicrously, but she didn't seem as concerned about its shape as finding something else in her purse.

"Oh, dear," she murmured to herself. She looked sideways

at me, about to say something, then gave her head a little shake and looked back down in her bag.

With some urgency, she looked up in the other direction at a slightly younger construction worker who was smoking an unfiltered Camel.

He turned toward her suddenly and gave her a very big smile. "Do you need a light?" he asked.

She nodded, embarrassed, and he flicked his lighter, producing a huge flame. She jumped back a little and laughed nervously as she leaned toward the fire.

"Thank you," she said primly, inhaling her crooked cigarette. The big, burly man sighed and closed his eyes momentarily in the breeze. When he opened them, he smiled at the distant skyline.

"Sure is beauty-ful," he said.

"Yes, it is," she answered. She seemed surprised that the words had come out of her mouth.

Then he walked away, and she looked like she wanted to call out after him. Instead, she turned back to the rail.

He was back in a few minutes with two coffees.

"Regular, no sugar," he said matter-of-factly as he handed her a cup. "Right?"

I don't think he saw her amazement as she nodded, but I did. She fumbled for words in the ensuing conversation, and he patiently waited for her to find them. I noticed the kindness on his face as he smiled at her attempted witticisms. They strolled off the ferry together, in step, when we landed on Staten Island.

The ferry was then on its way back to Manhattan, and I

didn't want to get off it, ever. I rode back and forth three more times, mulling over the simplicity of things.

But I didn't have a crumpled pack of cigarettes in my bag, and I don't think *he* even smokes.

It is done! This morning I finally emancipated myself from that godforsaken restaurant which has for far too long been the proverbial albatross around my neck.

I was fearless. It was as if the spirit of Dale Carnegie was by my side whispering motivational mantras in my ear: "You can do it. Go on, go on, make that change!"

I really had every intention of softening the news of my abrupt departure by saying something to the effect of, "You know, I really liked this place much more at times than it may have seemed," but as I approached the manager, an overpowering whiff of his Eternity by Calvin Klein shot up my nostrils, and suddenly it was as if I was possessed by some evil former employee.

I opened my mouth and out jumped, "This place sucks. I'm outta here," and with a spin on my toes I was out the door.

My elation propelled my freshly unshackled soul downtown where I spent the afternoon riding between Manhattan and Staten Island on the ferry. (Which, incidentally, is a bored poor man's ticket to adventure. It only costs fifty cents and you can ride all day. It's sort of like a bargain-basement Carnival Cruise.) I must have ridden back and forth at least forty times, staring out at the shiny skyline in one direction and at a dingy suburbia surrounded by the sea in the other. Back and forth again and again with the wind blowing everybody around me off their feet as I held on to the railing, excited about leaving that snack shack in the dust, and only a bit nervous about the rest of my life.

For no reason apparently, I started out feeling deeply sad tonight. Jillian insisted we go to this very authentic Irish pub for a change after work, and I couldn't believe how strongly I regretted that I wouldn't see *him* tonight.

I slouched in a booth and wanted to cry. J.C. said I wasn't really sad—that I just wanted to be. It was the Irish music, he said. I don't know.

I sort of hated everyone in the place. The singer was a reddish gold version of Pa Ingalls—too winky and humble-smiley. (I don't mind it in *Pa*, just not in old Danny O'Flaherty.) All the customers were so . . . like an ad for tourism boards everywhere. Of course, ol' Danny chatted with everyone but us. In return, they sent up requests jotted on napkins. (No yelling out, please; the waitress had to shush us twice.)

Now, the waitress, *she* was a trip. A scrubbed-till-she-shined lass who utterly radiated as she gazed ecstatically at Danny "the god" O'Flaherty. Actually, everyone in that place was radiating.

Why am I being so cynical? On his breaks, Danny O'Wonder wandered over to the bar and strummed along with the local groupies, ever so patiently teaching them songs. ("C, A-minor, G, G . . ." he sang as he strummed.)

J.C. and I made up our own rap-influenced version: *"A, A-minor, B, B, G . . . but don't forget the letter P. And since we're singing about P, how about X, Y, and Z . . ."* Very dumb, but we got carried away and went on to incorporate Chunky Monkey ice cream in the lyrics (which I'd do *anything* to remember, but at that point, the beer-and-ibuprofen combo kicked in, and it's all lost to me). At any rate, we got very loud—too loud, I'm sure—which is probably why we received the snub from Danny O'Boy.

There seems to be some hyperreality principle at work in this city. Most places it's kind of weirdly funny—like the boy in the bow tie and tux shirt, who sat alone at the end of another bar last night and bought Jillian and I four beers each in ten minutes' time, without ever acknowledging our presence. Or like that woman in the Irish pub tonight, who turned to us with a smile full of hospitality and said: "I've just got to run to the ladies' room to take care of this headache. Everyone's entitled to a urine headache at one time or another."

How this city can make me end up laughing, though I don't know why, exactly, or for how long.

I have this new favorite way of sitting. It's not actually all that new, really. I mean, I didn't make it up, I just recently accepted it as a comfortable way of relaxing.

It's that way that only women are supposed to sit: with one leg crossed right over the other. I used to consciously sit with my legs spread as far apart as possible. I mean, when I was sitting, I was a man. Nobody was going to look at me and call me a sissy.

And then, sort of overnight, I just crossed my legs. Completely girlie! Boy, was it comfortable.

Crisscross, crisscross, I love to cross my legs!

The glamour of my new career choice in this restaurant is beginning to tarnish. I keep waiting to develop that hard-skinned, cynical New Yorker quality that I admire so in those ancient red-haired coffee-shop waitresses, the ones who scream "Shut up!" to customers and cooks alike. Instead, my lower lip still trembles every time someone has to ask a second time for a glass of water.

Still, there's always the entertainment factor of this job to consider: like the Harley-Davidson couple who came in yesterday. I met them at the door to seat them—he had a weathered face and a salt-and-pepper beard; she was stocky and tough and looked all of sixteen. I greeted them with the universal restaurant line—"Smoking or non?"—and he answered, "Non." So I led them back to a booth in that section, except only he followed me. The girl remained planted right in the doorway. As soon as we turned around to look at her, she belted out a contralto credo across the almost full restaurant: "Daddy, I *smoke*."

I caught J.C.'s eye from across the room and we lost it. None of our customers had even a chance of service in the next five minutes because we were completely incapacitated with laughter. After we recovered, we spent the rest of the shift discussing their relationship: Was he her daddy or was he her "daddy"?

It's been a full month since I last talked to Joe. That is a definite record, and I believe I can safely say that we are now history. Our crazy love affair is only a memory now, and it is time for me to deal with the one person I really love to avoid: myself.

No more games, baby, this life thing is serious stuff. No hiding behind that Joe character anymore and heaping the blame on him. He's no longer an issue. What's done is done (finally), and though it is slightly sad, it is also a time to kick up the heels, clap the hands, and make a toast to new-found freedom.

Love has been a losing game for me for years now, man. It's time to focus on what really matters. (What's that?) Because it's obvious after numerous attempts at romance that it's not what I'm cut out for.

I'm tired of not having sex with people who I'm sup-posed to, goddammit, and I'm sick of disgruntled men run-ning around my apartment collecting their things and taking back gifts.

NO MORE!

From now on, sex will be a treat and will be had only with that special someone whom I will have no intention of ever seeing or speaking to again.

What Joe does now is of no concern to me. I wish him well and good luck in his pursuit of romance. See ya, Joe. I wanted to love you forever, but some things just weren't built to last.

A new waitress trailed today.

Blonde. Tall. Slim, with a great body, I suppose, if you notice those things. The guys in the restaurant sure did—even J.C., who I thought would have been exempt since he's gay, but he told me gay guys notice bodies, ALL bodies, a thousand times more than anyone else on earth.

The way they talked about her (and in front of me) made me sick. It sounds like jealousy, I know, but it's not, exactly. It appalled me that they just don't want to know any *more* of her than what they see. I'm now filled with the huge torture of wishing guys would look at *me* like that, and yet knowing that if they did, I'd hate them for that exact reason.

I guess a part of me can't help but think if I looked like her, I wouldn't be standing around just *watching* the guy from Z.

She's nice, I suppose, but I have no desire to really find out. Their talk has poisoned me, too, since I'm behaving the same way, but for different reasons. She carries herself with a certain self-satisfied knowledge that they're talking about her, which makes her kind of a traitor, in my eyes.

J.C. accusingly said that I would go out of my way to befriend any homeless person or someone who was ugly, but that I am prejudiced against anyone who looks like a model. I protested, but I think he may be right.

When I was little, I sometimes used to wish everyone was blind—not to the sky and grass and water, but to each other.

4. I wish I could be as happy as others seem to be.

Almost never...............................1
Sometimes...............................2
Often...............................3
Almost always...............................4

5. I feel like a failure.

Almost never...............................1
Sometimes...............................2
Often...............................3
Almost always...............................4

6. I get in a state of tension and turmoil as I think over my recent concerns and interests.

Almost never...............................1
Sometimes...............................2
Often...............................3
Almost always...............................4

7. I feel secure.

Almost never...............................4
Sometimes...............................3
Often...............................2
Almost always...............................1

8. I have self-confidence.

Almost never...............................4
Sometimes...............................3
Often...............................2
Almost always...............................1

9. I feel inadequate.

Almost never...............................4
Sometimes...............................3
Often...............................2
Almost always...............................1

10. I worry too much over something that does not matter.

Almost never...............................1
Sometimes...............................2
Often...............................3
Almost always...............................4

scoring

Add up the numbers under your answers to th
careful to notice that some of the rows of n
others go down.) The higher your total, the m
ety dominates your life. Adult men and wome
ferent scores on average, with women ben
anxious generally.

If you scored 10 or 11, you are in the low
terms of anxiety.

If you scored 13 or 14, you are in the low
If you scored 16 or 17, your anxiety level
If you scored 19 or 20, your anxiety level
fifth percentile.

If you scored 22 to 24 and you are male, y
around the ninetieth percentile.

If you scored 24 to 26 and you are female, w
around the ninetieth percentile.

If you scored 25 and you are male, your gr
ninety-fifth percentile.

If you scored 27 and you are
female, your anxiety level is at
the ninety-fifth percentile.

yo

If your score
or above, an
with the qua
do not feel ea
You can almo
cant improvem
your anxiety lev

If your score
percentile or ab
anxiety is paraly
fended, it is en
you should prob
thing about it.

If your score is
that anxiety is
as paralysis or in
nobody believe t
of lowering your a
a rate that com
question below, see p

I'm afraid of a lot of things and always have been. When I was a kid, I was scared to death of Sister Mary Ralph and her multiplication tables. For the life of me, I could never remember those things, and Sister took great pleasure, I'm sure, in making me stand before the class each day and stumble through the tables, knowing full well I would fail at the exercise. I'm not sure if it was stage fright or what, but every day I was a wreck as I waited to be called upon, knowing that as soon as my butt left my chair, the numbers would leave my head.

Each day I was accused of not studying and each day I'd end up going to the school nurse with a stomachache. Eventually it got so bad that Mom had to take me to the doctor and I was given pills to "soothe my nervous stomach."

I found out later that they were only sugar pills and that the pain had all been in my head. I would have sworn that the pain was in my ass and that it went by the name of Sister Mary Ralph. Imagine being so stressed out as a kid. It's a shame. I have to be fair, though; I wasn't singled out in class—there were several of us who were scared shitless by Sister Mary Mathematics.

It's funny how time can change what we're afraid of. Lately what I fear most is that I'll go bald before I have a chance to have distinguished-looking gray hair.

My head is lead, or might as well be since it's immobile, inside and out. I must have finally surpassed the number of brain cells you can kill and still be able to halfway function.

Nothing felt right about last night from the start. Even the air seemed determined to wrap its sticky tail around my face with the intention of suffocating me. I had to practically bribe everyone to get them to go to Z with me. (A strange sort of bribe that only the vampirish could come up with: *They* made *me* drink the libation of their choice—the last shot in the Mezcal bottle, including its occupant.)

It seems that, without letting me in on it, everyone else has suddenly decided that Z is officially a drag now. Yeah, it really appeared that way last week when J.C. was dancing on the bar and Jillian had every guy in the place calling her by a different name. It was Nick, surprisingly, who came to my rescue. He said he wanted to see what he'd been missing while he was wasting all that time with Doreen.

With a buildup like that, I don't care what kind of magical liquid you've just poured down your throat, the night is bound to be a letdown.

As we walked past the bouncer into the club, something like house music was playing, and there were actually *couples* out on the small dance floor. Couples who see nothing but each other and hold hands while dancing. They tend to run all the solitary and group dancers off the floor, and they are so absorbed at being part of a couple that they act like they own the place. Couples block the damn view of the people who *need* to make connections out there.

I sat at a corner table by myself and started to brood, but I knew that there was one face that would uplift me instantly. I craned my neck and tuned in to the black-clad motion in front of me: The prospect was as dead as the stifling air. J.C. passed by, holding a double in each hand, apparently checking out the scene with no better luck than me.

I saw Nick and Jillian talking together at the bar; then, like a flash-forward, they were entering a bathroom together. J.C. had made another circle around the room and stopped by my table this time.

"Gee, what a groovy place," he gushed in an impressive Marcia Brady. "Whose swell idea was this anyway?"

"Jan's," I said sullenly.

"Have you had enough already?" he asked, then switched into Southern Belle. "Or do you want to remain here on the vine, waiting for your fine gardener to come along and pluck you?"

I almost gave in and smiled. Almost. Then it hit me: What if I never saw *him* again? What if he had decided this place was a drag, too? What if he'd moved? Disappeared? I felt strongly, strangely, utterly desolate. I had nothing, and he'd been something, in my mind, at least.

With sudden steel resolve, I found myself headed straight toward the bartender. I was going to try to get any information I could about *him*—I didn't care how flaky it sounded. ("You know, the guy who stares into space and dances around it.")

"Hey. *Hey.*" J.C.'s voice, very irritated, behind me. "Where is everyone?"

I turned around.

The moment had left me; I wasn't going to ask anyone anything anymore.

"They're in the bathroom."

"*They*—together? Without me?" J.C. was really miffed. "Great. I'm out of here."

He left just as Jillian and Nick emerged, quite oblivious to me. I watched the expressions on Nick's face change in slow motion and heard Jillian's low laugh.

"I'm gonna regret this tomorrow," Jillian whispered as she passed me on her way out with Nick.

Not me. If you never *do* anything, you never have anything to regret.

I feel I could use a good soul-cleansing just about now. Perhaps I could submerge myself in a vat of holy water or maybe hop on a plane and head on over to Lourdes for a little sacred sponge bath. If what they told me in school is correct, my soul must be very dark indeed and only a miracle can save me now.

I'm feeling as if my actions of the past eight or nine years may—if what they say is true—cause a little problem when I try to march on in through those pearly gates. This past weekend alone might qualify as the one that keeps me out of the promised land.

I went to a party with Kevin, and as luck would have it, not only were beverages provided, but this generous queen was passing around tray after tray of coke. When I pointed it out to Kevin, he sort of got all bug-eyed and serious and said something about "desperate idiots" and "the excess of our shallow world."

On that note, I left him standing under a photo of two men holding a woman over their heads, with a caption that read, THE ONE WITH THE MOST WINS.

As is my nature, I made a beeline for the coffee table where a few guys were doing lines and discussing Sondheim and Fosse. Since I have no interest in Broadway, I just made myself comfortable and dove in.

I made it home two hours ago and found a note from Kevin which read: "If you want to kill yourself, I won't try to stop you, but I will not allow you to do so while you're my roommate. I think you should find another place soon. I'm sorry, and I hope you get help."

Well, needless to say, I feel like a piece of shit anyway

from not sleeping since Friday, and then to get a note from my friend, making me out to be some kind of junkie . . . It's all too much.

I'm not claiming to be an angel, and I do know I'm guilty of the occasional binge just like anybody else, but I am not a fucking junkie. It will be good for me to get away from Kevin anyway. He is definitely getting too uptight to deal with. I wish I could fucking rest, but I'm still wired. I think I still have a Valium in my desk.

All right, maybe he has a point, but it all seemed like such fun two nights ago.

Every time I wear this black-and-white shirt, printed with skulls of various sizes, the night turns on me. Even on the day I got it (for two dollars on St. Marks Place), J.C. and I were later insulted by the infamous Starr Booty.

Last night I wore it with cutoffs to Z. Jillian suddenly doesn't go out anymore, and since J.C. had a date, I went alone. I think I was secretly hoping this would be my chance to actually talk to the Z-man, but somehow I knew in my heart he wasn't going to be there either.

I danced around by myself for a while, trying very hard to enjoy the anonymity of knowing no one, but ended up feeling so invisible I thought I would disappear. I began to wonder what I was even doing there; not just tonight but every night of the entire nocturnal summer.

It made me think of summers when I was a kid. Jeannie and I would linger out in the backyard as long as we possibly could, well after dark, until Mom called us inside. Then we'd fall hard into sleep, satisfied we'd stolen that extra bit of day not usually entitled to us.

I was just ready to leave Z when "Ballroom Blitz" came on. No way, never ever, could I walk out on such a dancing opportunity. This seventies-looking guy with a beard was dancing next to me and seemed to be enjoying the song as much as I was. It occurred to me that maybe we were the only two people in the room who appreciated it—everyone else looked nineteen.

When the song was over he turned to me and said something I didn't quite catch. Why didn't it surprise me that he had an accent?

He asked again, "What is the word for, not 'death,' but like that?"

I rambled off a whole list—killed, deceased, passed away, to which he kept shaking his head—before it struck me that this was a little bit strange. So I started to walk away, but he moved in front of me, waving his arms as he kept saying, "Not 'death' but . . . ?"

"Life?" I asked dubiously, feeling like I was playing a version of Password which had rules I didn't quite know.

He shook his head hard, his eyes fixed on my chest.

It was definitely time to go.

Then I suddenly remembered the shirt I was wearing.

"Skull?" I asked, pointing to one of them. He grinned and nodded happily.

Then he composed himself, and spoke to me in a formal tone, as if the preceding conversation hadn't just occurred.

"You have such a benevolent face," he said.

I admit it's not a bad thing to have said to you, but my mood was so strange that I started brooding. Not that I wanted him to try to pick me up exactly, but any other female in the world, alone in a bar, would have been told she's beautiful or sexy or irresistible. And here I was, with this guy form Hungary or something telling me I have a *benevolent* face.

"Why, with such a face, do you wear that skull shirt?"

I wasn't about to go into it with him. Even without a language barrier, he wouldn't have understood. Anyway, who was he to question how I dressed? Did I point out to him that his tacky corduroy shirt was about twenty years out of date?

So I left the club without answering, thinking maybe I should go pierce a hole in this benevolent nose of mine.

I went to see Randy's kitchen today. He called and said he'd like me to have a look around so that everything isn't completely unfamiliar to me on the first day I come in to work.

When I got there, he was on the phone and motioned for me to have a seat. I looked around while I was waiting, and the place seemed pretty cool. It's a big space—there is one center area for working, and the rest of the room is cluttered with mixers and pots and pans and other cooking paraphernalia. When he got off the phone, Randy came over to where I was waiting and, instead of showing me around, started asking me all sorts of questions about my gym and my socks and other things that have very little to do with cooking. I said that I thought he had wanted me to see the kitchen, and he answered with, "Well, this is it. You've seen it. Let's go to lunch."

So we went out to eat, and I filled him in on myself. I asked him a few questions about cooking, again reminding him that I can't even make Cream of Wheat.

"You worry too much. It'll be fine, I promise."

So we left the restaurant, and I walked home thinking, "All right, I won't worry. It's your business and if you're not worried, I'm not worried."

I did stop by the library, though, and checked out a book called *The Idiot's Guide to the Kitchen*. Not that I think I'm an idiot, mind you, but I'm beginning to wonder if he might be.

J.C. and I got on the subway last night. He'd just been told that he had to shave off the goatee he'd started to grow. The restaurant has no formal rule about appearance that we've ever heard of, but now, out of the blue, they object to his "look."

With this sour thought in mind, we got on the train together. At the next stop, these four businessmen got on the train and sat across the aisle from us. They looked like high-school football players twenty years later—now squeezed into their corporate uniforms instead of their athletic ones. They were so superior in their attitude that they even acted like they owned the train.

This guy with really long gray hair and sunglasses sat down next to one of them, completely minding his own business.

The *looks* this one businessman shot that guy were incredible. He'd jerk his head toward him, roll his eyes, then turn back to his buddies with a disgusted expression. Oh, those lucky elites are such better human beings.

They were picking out all of the "freaks" on the train and mocking them with their eyes. They even looked at us a few times.

As the train pulled into Times Square and they gathered their briefcases, one of them brilliantly said, "We're off—like a prom dress!"

If that's real life, then I'd rather be a freak. I swear I once heard my Z-man say something to the effect that now and then you have to do something shocking to weed out all the idiots who would actually *judge* you based on such bullshit.

It must be around four in the morning, though I wouldn't know because my clock became mysteriously unplugged the day before yesterday. I have yet to plug it back in. I feel like I'm living on the edge: Will I or won't I wake up in time for work? And if I don't, will I care? I'm decidedly unexcited about my new career choice, so going there at all, let alone on time, hasn't been one of my biggest concerns of late.

It's wild that my moving came so suddenly. Kevin was, as they say, "over me" in the biggest way. It's strange that he suddenly became so concerned with my behavior and how it was affecting his life. I knew I shouldn't have become his friend all those years ago.

So here I am in the late-night hours, trying to clear my head with a pen instead of clogging it with a drink. I guess I think that if I keep doing this, I will get over some of this shit. Sometimes, it really seems to work. I start to write, and suddenly things make sense.

Or at least more sense than they did when all I did was think, think, think. And anyway, I guess writing is really just talking to myself, which I like. I like the comfort of knowing exactly what I mean. No explaining or clarifying. That was the problem between me and Kevin. For years we didn't talk about anything and it worked. And then, out of nowhere, he starts to change and wants to talk about everything all the time, and I was like, Whoa, what's going on here? What happened to the boy I knew? The one who was as disinterested in life as I was?

How I fucking wish there was one person on this planet who truly "got" me. One other soul who could almost read my mind and almost feel what I feel. And I would try as hard as I possibly could to understand him, and the two of us would only need each other (and some beer and music). Ah, yes, total understanding—a definite fantasy. That to me would be bliss, bliss, complete bliss.

I have that heavy and sore feeling in my chest, that feels like someone slept on top of me all night. I remember it from childhood, when my dog used to sleep on me—even though it hurt, there was something sweet in where the hurt came from. Now, I suppose, it comes from inhaling too many cigarettes.

At least that's what Jillian would be quick to point out. Since she's joined AA, Jillian has been littering the restaurant with all kinds of self-help pamphlets that pinpoint early warning signs of assorted bad behavior more enthusiastically than any evangelical minister. Somehow it isn't sinking into her head that all this stuff you're not supposed to do is all new to me. It doesn't quite seem fair that the wildest friend I've ever had would decide to mend her ways right after I made her my acquaintance.

Still, I'm trying to be supportive of her, which isn't easy. She marches into the restaurant and announces things like, "Where are our lives going? What kind of a dead-end job are we stuck in?" (*She* may be stuck; I just lowered myself in here for a change of scenery.) Her tone dangerously hints at suggesting a four-week course: Word Processing for Dollars.

All of a sudden, I don't want to be clumped together with her anymore. Two weeks ago, when she called us "wild-ass degenerates," it was okay. But when it comes to her search for a sunnier, more lucrative tomorrow, I'll remain here in the shadows—where there's a good view of a god on the dance floor down the block.

On my way home from work today, I stopped and had my palm read. This woman was sitting in front of the Nightingale Bar on Second Avenue. She had an orange crate standing on end, and she was sitting in a Laz-E-Boy recliner. How she got the chair there, I don't know, and I didn't bother asking because I thought not knowing made it all the more interesting.

I sat down on the ground next to her and she took my palm. For a long while she stared at it, occasionally glancing down into my eyes.

She started out by saying that she saw a long period of solitude, during which time I would experience many hardships and feel very alone. Thank you very much, Little Gypsy Sunshine! Just when I was about to ask her to stop attacking me with visions of my bleak future, she spit out something about looking into Lufthansa Airlines.

It seems that I somehow have a tremendous amount of stock in that particular company. She couldn't tell me how this came about—she just assured me that she was never wrong and that first thing in the morning, I should check on it.

"It will make your loneliness easier to take," she said as I was leaving.

Where she got her information, I don't know, but I do have half a mind to march into the Lufthansa office on Fifth Avenue tomorrow and fire the entire staff.

My mind seems to be tuning in to the most disturbing things lately—or is there a sudden acceleration of bizarre events surrounding me these days?

I was walking up Second Avenue today, toward the carnival on 14th Street, when I was enveloped by its fantastic overspill. It was around noon so there were almost more pedestrians than vehicles on the street. Just as I was about to step off the curb, a clear voice emerged from the traffic.

"Hey, you!"

Instinctively I stiffened and tried to glance around without appearing to be the one summoned. Something about this catcall was different. The strong voice sounded again.

"Yeah, you in the white shirt."

I realized I wasn't the target. I was wearing a black shirt. Then it registered that the voice belonged to a *woman*.

I looked around behind me to try to locate its owner, but I saw only a skinny guy with a straggly mustache sidestepping an old woman in an armchair. He nervously looked back over his shoulder. He was wearing a dirty white T-shirt.

The voice carried all over the street again: "That's so MANLY, you're a real man. Yeah, *you*, what a MAN."

The jeer sounded insane, and I felt sorry for the nervously approaching man who was running away from the anonymous taunt. I felt a little guilty for belonging to my particular sex at that moment, and a little angry that some militant feminist should be an immediate *cause* of misogyny all around us.

"Ooh, *manly*," she continued. Finally I located a woman

about my age on a plain one-speed bike, weaving in and out of traffic and parked cars, following the man in the dirty white T-shirt. She looked completely normal; in fact I kind of thought she might be one of the checkout clerks at the A&P.

"Feeling a little nervous?" she yelled as the man shrank into his shoulders. "Good."

He tried to cross the street, but she cut him off with a swerve of her bike.

"Does your mother know you do this? She'd be so proud of her little MAN."

He was practically running by now, only a row of parked cars between him and his relentless agitator.

"Yeah, YOU, white T-shirt. Grabbing a woman like that, you think that makes you MANLY?"

My stomach turned upside down.

The guy I had been sympathizing with turned and lunged toward the woman on the bike. How had I missed the vicious-ness that was all over his face?

"Shut up!" he screamed, and shook with rage as she grace-fully dipped her bike away from the curb.

The sudden screech of car tires and a couple of shouts from the street went right through me; I had no desire to see whatever tragedy lay out there in the street, but some-thing in me had to look. I turned in time to see the back of the woman, finally riding away across 14th Street. Her "victim," fists tightly clenched, was screaming at the driver of the car that had obviously swerved to miss him. At least no one was hurt.

I then caught sight of the real victim, a girl, frozen, with her

arms wrapped all around her body, trying to keep whatever
was left of herself together.

   The whole incident left me feeling numb. I couldn't help
but wish I could pick up the phone and call the one person
who might be able to fill the emptiness I felt.

Idea #3

I've written a letter to Paloma Picasso asking for a donation
to my decorate-my-apartment fund. I explained that I had
recently moved and am short on artwork. I thought maybe
she might have some sketch of her father's just lying
around, perhaps one that isn't so terrific, one that maybe
she doesn't care for all that much.

I plan to write to other artists and their families and
make the same request. Who knows?—something might
come of it.

Although when I was young, I wrote to Mary Tyler
Moore and asked if she might be able to help my recently
divorced mother. I never received a response. I suppose
that's the chance one has to take when asking for handouts.

It's been a full fifteen days and six hours since I've seen *him*. That's probably why I'm so peevish. Even the smallest things are getting to me—like the way some guys sit on the subway, with their legs sprawled wide open just like they're lounging on their living-room Laz-E-Boys watching "Wide World of Sports."

When you try to squeeze into an open seat beside one of them, and that knee of steel won't budge, no matter how many times you say "Excuse me" or bump into it, it's more than irritating—it sucks.

Today, I felt like I just couldn't take it anymore. On the subway, loads of people were standing, and from my place on the pole, I noticed this one guy who was guilty of that same macho leg positioning. An older woman at the other end of the seats asked loudly if everyone could move down just a bit, and the majority of the row scooted en masse. The older woman then took her seat, but didn't even have enough room to sit all the way back. In the midst of all of those pressed-together knees, edge-of-the-seat postures, and other attempts to minimalize body mass, was that set of arrogant, wedged-open legs.

Not to wish the guy any harm, exactly, but I found myself thinking anyone who pushes his body parts upon others deserves to lose them.

I've come up with a new plan to smother my feelings of loneliness. I got a cat.

I saw a sign in the Laundromat and called about it. A not-overly-friendly man told me that he'd had this cat for nine years but woke up the other morning and decided he was "sick of looking at the fat old thing." I told him I would take the cat without seeing it. I felt like it was my duty to rescue him from this animal-lover-gone-mad. I picked him up somewhere on Third Avenue. The man told me to meet him on the street because "I don't like strangers knowing where I live, and besides, I don't want you bringing that thing back here if you decide you hate it." Charming exchange.

So now I'm the proud owner of a big old black-and-white cat whom I've named Doug. The former owner said he never had time to think of a name. (I can understand that—what's nine years?)

I'm hoping this cat will make this living-alone thing easier to take. He immediately went to sleep when I brought him here and hasn't moved since. I don't know how stimulating our relationship will be, but I don't antici-pate any arguments.

Jillian coerced me into going to a job fair with her. I have adamantly refused to go to a job *counselor* because even though I know they're not real psychiatrists or anything, it sounds perilously close to seeing a therapist. I really don't need *that* right now.

A job fair seemed safe enough, especially since the restaurant has been less than fulfilling lately. I've been blocking out the feeling that's started to hit me in the middle of the night— that I may want more from life than tacos and dark nightclubs— because I realize I can't go back to my other life.

It's not that this sabbatical of mine from real life has thrown me off course, but for the first time in my life, I no longer *have* a course. I've neatly and irrevocably renounced it. I don't know for what, right now, which maybe should be the cause of some concern.

I guess that's why I let Jillian drag me here, to look at booths filled with information like starting my own miniature goat farm.

One of the booths featured a free career test, so Jillian and I both took it. It was quick, and they gave you the results about fifteen minutes later. It really felt like high school. Jillian is bubbling next to me because *hers* says she should be an international spy. At this point I'm certain they will try to sentence me to a life of certified public accounting, but, thankfully, I'm wrong. It seems my most compatible career choice is running a bed-and-breakfast.

Great. I'll remember that the next time I find a Victorian chalet for rent on Avenue A.

Today I thought about when I was in grade school and my mom used to quiz me the night before a spelling test. Every Tuesday night I would sit with her on our orange couch in our paneled family room and attempt to spell the words as she called them out to me. Spelling didn't come easy to me, and I used to get quite pissed when time and time again I would misspell the words.

One night we were going over the list and she gave me the word *yearn.* I repeated the word, "Yearn," and then spelled it u-r-i-n-e. Mom, usually so together, found this particular misspelling too funny to skip over without comment. She explained my mistake to me and I remember the two of us laughing until we almost produced that word I'd spelled on the family-room floor.

I also had a very difficult time with math and could never remember what integers were. I always confused integers with dirigibles. And even then I was totally fucked because I thought dirigibles were numbers and integers were some sort of prehistoric animal, the whole while leaving out airships completely (thinking they were all just Goodyear blimps).

Which leads me to today. I saw the blimp three times.

But the point of this whole thing is that I now know how to spell *yearn,* I know the difference between dinosaurs and fractions, and its seems all that I can remember from my days in school are all the things I couldn't remember when I was in school.

I saw one of those double-decker red buses like they have in London today. I was waiting to cross Second Avenue as it drove by, and I saw what appeared to be a bunch of middle-aged Midwesterners taking me in as part of the colorful East Village scenery. As they drove by I noticed a big sign on the side of the bus saying they needed tour guides.

I wasn't sure I'd love a job like that, but I could imagine *him* stepping on the bus one day, in a mood to be a tourist in his own city. And there I would be, giving the tour-guide spiel; it would be my *job* to talk to him then.

I called the number, just out of curiosity. The man who answered didn't even listen to my impressive history of public speaking. He just told me in a monotone that all the positions had already been filled. I hung up the phone, morosely certain that the newly hired tour guides were timid bioengineering majors who were lousy public speakers and not nearly as qualified for the job as me.

The experience shook me up a little, though, thinking it might not be so easy to get back to a real life when I finally decide I want to. All of a sudden it occurred to me that people are not necessarily where they are because they *want* to be; it's not always going to be up to me to decide the entire course of my life.

I don't know if I find this exciting or terrifying.

Had I lived in New York during the seventies, I seriously doubt that I would be alive today. I remember reading stories about the decadent goings-on at Studio 54 and wanting so badly to drop out of school to run to New York and take part in all the glorious debauchery that was going on. I had daydreams of doing drugs in the bathroom with Calvin Klein and doing the Bump on the dance floor with Liza Minnelli. And I remember cursing my parents in my head for keeping me unborn for so long. So I missed out on the seventies in New York; I made it here just in time to see the sad tail end of an era which wound up costing a lot of people more than they ever imagined. Still, my friends and I would make furious nightly attempts at having the party that would outblast them all.

Last night I went out. Not so unusual except for the fact that I didn't want to. The thought of being with people didn't appeal to me, but it was as if I had no power over myself, like I was being led around by an invisible hand. I went from bar to bar—drinking a beer, playing a few songs on the jukebox and a game of pinball, and then I'd find myself on the street, walking toward another place. Automatic pilot.

I've always been good at spotting drug dealers in a crowd, and it wasn't long before I was in a bathroom, spooning coke into my nose. And it wasn't too long after that that I was talking to some guy, and we were out the door and on the way to his apartment.

He lived uptown, so we got a cab on First Avenue and rode in that annoying nervous silence when two people know they're only waiting to have sex. We got to 47th

Street and his apartment. Inside, he asked if I wanted a drink, and then he started to cut some coke on the table.

I watched him for a while in silence and then he motioned for me to do a line. I did, and while I had my head down to the table, he put his hand on my shoulder. I sat back and turned toward him, but as he moved in to kiss me, I stood up. I wasn't losing myself. I was all too aware that I didn't know this guy, and I was pretty damn sure he didn't remember my name.

"I gotta go," I said, walking toward the door.

"What are you talking about?" he said. "We just got here and we've got all this stuff. Relax. Sit down."

By this time I had walked to the window, through which it seemed I could see the entire city, and in which I could also see a reflection of my tired self. I turned and only said, "No," and left. I walked home wired as hell and haven't slept yet.

I'm pissed at myself and I'm fucking tired. Tired of nights like last night where it seems I'm on a mission to destroy myself. For all I know, some action of mine six years ago has had me lined up for death ever since, and last night, for some reason, that seemed fucked up.

I feel like a fly with one broken wing, buzzing like mad, able only to go in circles on the ground. Buzzing and circling like crazy, waiting for some big boot to smash me.

I was thinking about the time a couple of years ago I went with Jeannie for her job interview at Vidal Sassoon. I had just helped her move to San Francisco (where she would remain for four days) and she was utterly broke. Even though Jeannie had traveled all over the world by herself, when it came to alien situations like getting real jobs, she couldn't do it on her own so she begged me to go along.

When she went in, I sat outside the salon on a cement wall on Post Street, thinking how perfect Jeannie would be for Vidal Sassoon. When she'd lived in London, she got to be a regular groupie of the Vidal Sassoon salon over there, since she had her hair asymmetrically cut or bleached or fringed every other week. I'd seen her pictures of the Sassoon gang once—a bunch of spacey, punk-styled street urchins who looked surprisingly sweet.

Jeannie seemed to be in her interview forever; I spent ten-minute chunks of time strolling around Union Square, dodging cable cars and pedestrians.

Finally, she emerged from the glossy building front and stormed up the cement steps to my roost.

"Was it horrible?" I asked, fulfilling my purpose for being there.

"There were about twenty people applying," she said indignantly.

I murmured something like "Well, then!" with sympathetic indignation to match hers.

"And they offered it to *me*," she said, even more hotly.

I repeated, "Well, then!"—brightly this time, but confused.

"They want me to wear a *suit*." She spat the word out.

The rip on the thigh of her black tights shot down another two inches.

"Maybe you could get a sort of funky suit?" I started to offer, but dropped it as she glared at me.

Two weeks later she met a handsome Brazilian, eloped, and now travels back and forth to South America with him.

Now that I've seen (but not really met) *my* dream man— why can't things work out the same for me?

I have yet to leave my apartment today. I've been lying here listening to one song off each CD (I'm up to "Edge of Seventeen" by Stevie Nicks) and counting the roaches in each of my roach motels. So far, the trap in the bathroom is ahead by eight, and that, I must admit, confounds me. What is it exactly that these roaches went into my bathroom looking for? I have three opened bags of Doritos and a Little Debbie Nutty Bar in the cupboard, and the trap in there has only caught two roaches. Go figure.

I thought that Doug might aid in my battle of the bugs, but every time I point out a roach to him, he just stares at it. I tried yelling, "Kill it, kill it!" but he only looks at me and then goes back to sleep. He's proven to be no trouble whatsoever, and I have found myself forgetting that I am even a pet owner until I go in the bathroom and see the litter box. Shitty little cat. It's nice having another heartbeat in the apartment, although I could go for a purr every now and then.

I've been thinking of getting a black cat tattooed on my person somewhere, but just where, I'm not sure. I've wanted a tattoo for some time, but it has to be the right one. I don't want to be one of those millions of people with the li'l devil seared into my skin forever, only to wake up on the morning of my fifty-sixth birthday unable to go on because of an adolescent impulse from years earlier. Tattoos are a major decision, man. I'm always seeing middle-aged men with *Lynda* or something tattooed on their arms and the color's all faded and you just know that the poor guy and Lynda were history years ago, yet there he is, stuck with an ugly name on his arm for all eternity.

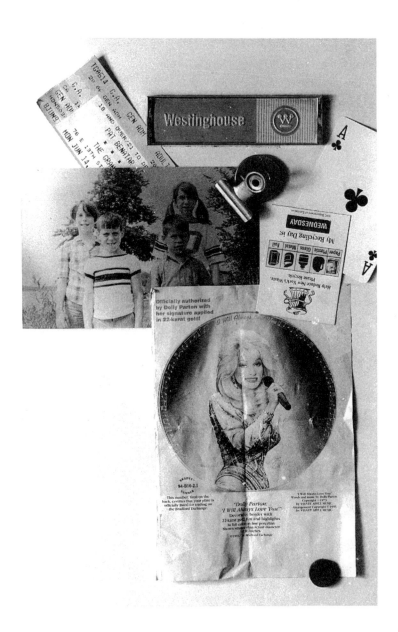

All my tattoo talk must be a result of my Jack Daniel's orgy last night. I always feel a little wrong-side-of-the-tracks after a J.D. drunk. Anyway, I suppose I should venture out into the world before I develop bedsores.

Maybe I'll go to the gym so I can compare myself to all those nondrinking bodybuilders. That ought to put me in a good mood.

I'm crazy, I tell you. But as time passes, I find I'm learning to live with it.

Today I was seriously reconsidering picking up my real life where I left off, after an irate customer haughtily informed me that *she'd* never been a "fucking waitress." But then I remembered the day at the ad agency when I reached the point where I couldn't take it anymore either. Not "didn't want to," but *couldn't*.

Some flu or general ennui had most of the secretaries out of the office that particular Friday, so we "assistants" (that is, the *female* portion of us) were called upon to "pitch in" and help out with the secretarial duties.

That's how I found myself answering phones for Jeremy Kobb, the head of the mysterious Research Department. No one really knew what he did.

I had anticipated that I wouldn't know exactly what was going on in this new-to-me department, but nothing could have prepared me for the strangeness of the day. After numerous hang-ups when I cheerily answered, "Research," I finally heard a voice at the other end of one of the calls—a woman with a heavy accent asking for "Justine." I looked on the department's roster. There was no Justine. I told the woman she had a wrong number but she kept insisting.

Jeremy Kobb happened to be passing by as I suggested she check with the main receptionist, and he hissed, "Who is it?" at me. I shook my head to indicate I was handling it, but he came right down in my face, hissing, "Who? Who?" I put the woman on hold and told him some crazy person was asking for a Justine.

Jeremy's face turned beet red and in a tone indicating that I was a complete moron, he told me *never* to say that anyone wasn't here, no matter *what* the name was. Then he marched in his office, shut the door, and took the call.

The day only got worse. At one point, he brought out those little forms for certified mail and took painstaking measures to instruct me h-o-w t-o f-i-l-l i-t o-u-t.

All I wanted to do was scream at him that I do have a college degree, but I was immediately ashamed of this sudden impulse of mine. Somehow I knew that wasn't really what this exercise was all about.

By the time the afternoon rolled around and he had asked me to sharpen all his pencils, I was ready to throw them in his face and remind him that I didn't even work for him, so wasn't he pushing it just a bit? But immediately I knew *that* wasn't the real point either.

I thought I was finally out of there; five-thirty on a Friday and I had pitched in as much as I possibly could. I had my coat on when the phone rang. I hesitated, wanting to get the hell out, but knowing I couldn't walk away from a ringing phone. I picked it up quickly—a chipper sales rep from California asked for "the boss."

Jeremy happened to walk by as I put her on hold so I told him about the call.

"Did she ask for me by name?" he asked, interrupting me. I'd already told him she hadn't.

He instructed me to take her number without telling her his name then rushed off to his office.

I was all the way down the hall, finally on my way home, when I heard him running to catch up with me.

"Well?" he demanded.

"Well what?"

"What did you say?"

I told him I took care of it as he'd instructed.

"No, no—*exactly* what did you say?" He was getting excited. "Did you give her my name?"

I heard The Tone loudly creeping into my voice, the tone that always got me grounded in high school.

"I *told* her *exactly* what *you said*—NOT your . . . *name*."

Then Jeremy Kobb stepped back.

"Whoa, girl," he said in an absolutely controlled voice, while actually pulling on imaginary reins. "Whoa."

I suddenly knew that *this* was it and that it had nothing to do with me, personally, or this Jeremy Kobb, vile as he was.

It was that I found myself smack in the middle of a world which still gives the reins to one person in order to hold another down, no different than a feudal lord riding a serf or a plantation master driving a slave. Why, I wondered, couldn't we all take care of ourselves?

Today at work, Randy showed me how to trim a fillet of beef. A vegetarian's nightmare, to be sure. The entire morning involved fondling cold red meat, pulling off fat and wiping up blood. Not glamorous.

I was able to feign interest until about eleven, after which I'm sure my sighs gave me away. I dealt with the same fillet all morning while Randy, chatting away like the happy butcher, handled the other five. After we finished cleaning and tying up the carnage, we moved on to crudités.

The afternoon mainly consisted of peeling, chopping, and blanching vegetables, and taking a "break" to make lunch for Randy and his friend Roger. (Nothing too difficult—tuna fish salad—and yet I resented it all day.)

I think it would be safe to say that my bad attitude is seeping into this job much earlier than I had anticipated. That's really too bad. I had such hopes that this job would not upset me for at least eight months, but as it turns out, it's just the same as the others—or maybe I'm the same as I've always been. Either way, when it comes down to it, just hand over the paycheck already.

I flushed some crack down my toilet tonight.

I hate to admit to the thrill it gave me, because, while I admittedly find some glamour in the whole drug-culture thing, I don't think I ever expected to have *crack* in my possession.

What I mean is, if some other drug found its way into my apartment—pressed into my hand tonight by some guy I met at the restaurant who is apparently a drug dealer, and who grabbed me and made me walk up the block with him whispering, "Just walk with me! I told them you're a cop!" If at that point, he had shaken my hand and passed on a bag of hash or shrooms or X, I probably would have entertained the idea that if *fate* has placed this in my hands . . . well, who am I to question fate?

I'm sure I would have deliciously considered trying it—and even if I hadn't done it, I know I would have *saved* it, storing it away with my old postcards and matchbooks and florescent plastic cocktail stirrers.

I would have had tantalizing daily peeks at it, poking it, sniffing it—waiting for what I knew would be the inevitable day to plunge into this whole dark world that I lean over so closely—just like the time when I was fourteen and working at Burger King, and I found a hypodermic needle when I was taking out the trash. I carried it around in my purse for weeks, getting a thrill every time I glimpsed it among my flavored lip glosses and Danielle Steel paperbacks.

But instead, it's *crack,* and I can't block out what I've seen crack do to its users:

That girl I first met a week ago, with the emaciated face and raving red eyes. She was standing in the doorway of my building again as I walked home yesterday. The *first* day I'd seen her there, her eyes had been clear as she implored me to loan her ten dollars so she could get to her job. I did, in the midst of her rushed promises that she would return it at eight o'clock that night. She didn't, but my buzzer had rung at midnight, and there she was with her wild red eyes and my ten dollars.

"Tell me the truth," she had said, "you didn't think I'd return it, did you?"

I replied, "Yes, of course," but she didn't believe me because no one has ever believed *her*.

Last night, the money I handed her was mostly because I couldn't look at her now twitching, strung-out face any longer. She made no promises to return *this* money.

She's the first dead person I've ever seen.

This morning, in the doorway of that closed-down sixties novelty shop on Avenue A, on my way to breakfast at the Odessa, I saw her for the last time. A homeless guy was skimming over her body with one of those full-size metal detectors that beachcombers use to look for money in the sand.

All I could think of was how pretty she looked with her eyes shut.

I'm wondering if heaven is cliquish. I mean, if I were to die of an accidental overdose before I made a name for myself down here on earth, could I still hang with Janis Joplin and River Phoenix up there? Or would they be off in their own corner laughing with John Belushi, leaving me to pass the time with corrupt businessmen who had done themselves in after being exposed as thieves, and unpopular teenage girls who couldn't handle not being on the cheerleading squad?

Last night, after a few swigs of tequila, I impetuously inhaled about a tablespoon of Ketamine and was immediately thrust into the darkest of K-holes. There was a lot of swaying and sweating and general incoherence, all of which only led up to the free vomit show I put on out on Second Avenue. I know I made it home because I'm here, but how I got here is another story, and one I fear I may never hear.

I've spent today flipping through *TV Guide* and eating Little Debbies while trying to piece together my journey home. No clue. One of these days I'm going to have to dig up my birth certificate and check to see if my middle name might not indeed be Trouble.

Last night I dreamed it was the eve of the big nuclear war. I haven't had a War dream since high school, back when TV shows were regularly interrupted with Special News Reports about invasions and rebellions and ousted dictators. Just hearing those words, "Special Report," put a special feeling of dread in the pit of my stomach—like how I always imagined I'd feel on the day that the Emergency Broadcast System's high-pitched test tone would be followed by the words, "This is *not* a test. This is a real emergency."

Anyway, in my dream, the event was scheduled to take place in this big stadium-type place that looked almost Athenian: white, with columns, up on a hill under an enormous sky.

The open-air stadium clearly offered a privileged view and the box seats guaranteed an elite shelter, leaving everyone inside strangely relaxed and calm. My family was seated there, so I felt free to move about, as if I were the hostess of some big social event. I kept running into old friends and acquaintances like it was a casual reunion or a rerun of my life.

As it got later and darker, I saw the guy from Z, realizing with a guilty pang that he was someone I'd long forgotten. We approached each other as we usually do in reality—cautiously, from across a distance—and his silent smile said more than any words could.

Then someone yelled, "There it is!" and through a large observation window, I saw a huge brown mushroom cloud on the horizon. Silhouettes of bodies flying through the air in slow motion were narrated by an anonymous anchorman: ". . . killed by a stray bullet"; ". . . it was probably AIDS"; ". . . mixed illegal substances with cold medicine . . ."

All of a sudden my dream seemed like I was *in* a bad

dream. I looked around to see if everyone was all right, but none of my old friends were there anymore. With great relief I did find my family in a church-basement type of place with the other survivors; everyone had bandages over their eyes.

All of the young men were gone, as if off to battle. I had always thought it would all be over in one flash, but I woke up with the feeling that maybe the Big War had evolved into ongoing daily explosions as relentless as any bomb.

One of my favorite tapes was repeatedly run over on First Avenue this afternoon. I was walking home from the gym and picking up stuff for lunch along the way. At the time of the incident, I had my backpack on, and I was holding a beefsteak tomato in one hand and a two-liter bottle of Dad's Root Beer in the other. I saw that the light was about to change on me, so I made a mad dash into the street, determined to make it to the other side.

Just as I was right smack in the middle of the street, I heard something hit the pavement. I wasn't sure at that point if I had lost something or if someone was hurling things at me from an unseen window. When I reached the curb on the other side of the street, a woman started yelling, "Hey! Hey! You dropped something."

When I looked back, there it was—my Patti Smith tape lying alone and unprotected in the street. I, of course, was just about to run and retrieve it when the light changed, and what seemed like every car in New York began one after another to drive over it.

I turned and walked in the direction of home, and I swear I could hear the sound of splintering plastic the whole length of the block.

Change is in the air.

A sense of the holiday season—my birthday and Halloween—hit me fully today as I was walking home from work. I was carrying the dozen roses (in almost perfect shape) that I had found in the Dumpster outside the restaurant, my first good omen in ages. Visions of my spectacular costume for J.C.'s upcoming party danced in my head. My real sight was partially and pleasantly impaired by the roses.

It was getting dark enough that I shouldn't have been able to recognize the approaching figure that I suddenly noticed about a block away. How could I *not* recognize, however, an image that has been carved into the inside of my eyelids from so many dreams? How was it possible that any other face could make such a precious shadow, that any other body could carry that particular face through space with that gliding walk?

It was *him* again, after all this time. Sent to me again by Destiny no doubt. As he got closer and closer to me (or did I get closer and closer to him? did I even move?), I felt myself shrinking behind the thorny forest in my arms. I peeked out long enough to see him glance curiously at the mask of flowers that was passing him on the street.

I now have a very strong sense that I have been given one last chance with him, and this time I'm not going to blow it.

Next time, I promised myself, the ashen twilight will witness what was meant to happen: Our eyes locked for a block, we'd finally reach speaking distance, and I wouldn't be able to hold back any longer.

"Happy Halloween!" I'd say, surprising both of us.

Before he'd even have a chance to absorb this momentous

event, I would have pulled out a single red rose from my bou-
quet.

"Happy Halloween," I'd repeat softly, handing him the
rose.

I wouldn't really know what his reaction would be; I'd
have already walked quickly away. I wouldn't see his reaction,
but another image would be carved on the inside of my eyelids: a joyous girl walking away from a bewildered (but
strangely elated) boy—walking away with a-dozen-minus-one
roses into the late-October sunset.

Randy was getting a little touchy today (and I'm not talking angry). He asked me to look at a recipe with him—he said he wanted to explain something about egg whites to me. I went and sat next to him on the sofa, and we began reading about angel food cake, in which egg whites play a very important part. So I'm sitting there, and all out of nowhere, Randy asks me what I do at the gym for my legs. As I never work out my legs, I answered, "Nothing," and he said (as he touched my leg perilously close to my crotch), "I can't believe that. It feels like there's something nice under your jeans."

I felt two things. The first was like he had just said some tacky line from a seventies porno movie, and the other was that this seemingly sweet guy who was helping me out with a great job was actually like everyone else.

It is, after all, going to be my birthday. If what I want more than anything else in the world is within my power to give myself, why shouldn't I? Why shouldn't I write an anonymous invitation (borrowing lyrics from an Anne Clark song) on the back of a postcard? Why shouldn't I then take it with me to Z early one evening and slip it into *his* jacket, which will no doubt be carelessly flung across the bar, while he is out on the floor, lost in his dance?

Why shouldn't I believe that the bartender who will obviously see me do it won't laugh at the absurdity of this awkward girl and later give me away to him?

Why shouldn't I cling to my secret inkling that even if he were to suspect who it came from, he'd still come to the party, shyly smiling behind his hesitation . . . ?

No! I don't want to wish for any outcomes or make up any endings. I just want a chance to finally let things *happen* between us—to be a participant, for once, instead of the perpetual observer, in this unreal life of mine.

Surprise, surprise, surprise! Gomer has a secret admirer. The thrill of it all! Someone out there amongst all the dancing drunks in the bar last night stuck a sweet little party invitation into the sleeve of my jacket. I suspect it's the bartender. There *is* a certain electricity between us each time he hands me a fresh Budweiser.

Ditch Day. I never did it when I was in school because that was back when I believed in everything too much to rebel. It was when I thought I respected the world but was actually afraid of it. But today—the white-gray sky, the damp air that's stuck endlessly beyond summer but not a real autumn day—it's all too stagnant to bear. When J.C. suggested ditching work for Coney Island, how could I resist? Besides, I've never been there.

Why is it that I'm always more attracted to places like this when they're deserted and seemingly dead? All the rides are frozen (some in midair); as a result *we* felt frozen.

We strolled along the streets of the area and were the sole customers of flea markets that reminded me (sharply) of Saturdays when I was a kid. How is it possible to so easily be back in another place and time while I'm so aware of the clarity of today?

Then we saw The Dress. It was a mint-condition 1960s cocktail dress, in the style of a twenties flapper dress—exactly what I had been visualizing for my Zelda Fitzgerald costume for J.C.'s party. I had to look perfect, absolutely perfect, in case he *did* respond to my invitation.

J.C., in one of his rare serious moments, stopped and said that I just *had* to get it. It was made for me, he felt. It *was* me.

I knew it, too. There was nowhere to try it on, so I just bought it. Now I'm back in my apartment, as if home from a magic-carpet ride, trying on the dress.

It's not just fine; it is perfect. I not only look good, I'm transformed. Cinderella tale come true, I'm practically dancing on air; why do I feel so much better not as me at all?

I was just walking around when I saw this 1962 Plymouth Dynamic for sale today on 9th Street. It is sea-foam green and the front seat is as big as my mom's living room. I had an incredible urge to buy it, speed to my apartment, pick up the cat, and drive right on out of this town. Never to return.

I dreamed I saw *him* again, as I usually see *him*—in the club, both of us staring without staring. Then, a hard, unhappy woman began to cruelly and loudly make fun of me. *She* had somehow seen our gazes (don't we realize the whole world can see them?) and singled me out.

She then gathered her two small daughters who had suddenly materialized at her side, and I knew (with that special dream-certainty) that these were *his* wife and children.

He held my gaze longer than usual as he turned to dutifully join them, and his eyes cried out for help, for understanding.

I turned to leave the room, to escape into the music, and as I crossed the threshold, he was there again, stopping only for a second on his way to somewhere else.

He almost spoke; we almost spoke. Our lips were frozen in the little *o*'s that would appear to anyone else to be surprise or disbelief or shock. How misinformed anyone else would have been, seeing this situation.

Then he was gone—and I was alone in my seat, waiting to hear the band again. But I no longer needed to escape into the music. The songs, I decided, would now be a celebration of my deep and long-awaited faith in him.

I later sensed him next to me again and his presence was no new excitement, but became the core of that whole and perfect joy that had already overtaken me earlier. When an already perfect joy exists, it seems that nothing can be added without making it burst. Its perfection, maybe, allows it to accommodate even more: HE TOOK MY HAND.

We did not *hold* hands; our hands wept, rejoiced, read each other, joined souls, made love, coexisted.

I woke up envying my hand.

I've been masturbating like a fiend as of late. It's so odd because it was never a big thrill for me in the past. I used to look upon it as the last resort, when for whatever reason I couldn't interest someone in spending a little time with me. But now it's entirely different.

Now it's me who can't be bothered. Lately, I can't muster up the energy to even think about going out and picking someone up, let alone actually doing it. It's like I've used up all my desire and lust, and nobody has even a slight chance of interesting me. Now I've turned to myself for relief, and let me tell you, I wish I would have tapped into this years ago. It's quick, easy, and dependable—gets the job done with minimal trouble and no conversation. I feel like a kid all excited about figuring something out for the first time.

Party night.

It seems like a hundred years ago since I started getting ready, stepping into my glass slippers with sky-high hopes, but it actually took only a few hours to completely annihilate Cinderella. I put on my magical Zelda Fitzgerald dress and had three glasses of wine (to calm down, not necessarily in celebration). Happy birthday to me.

I wondered why I felt so much better, so much more like who I really am, dressed like this. Maybe because Zelda had passion and romance and F. Scott? Maybe because dressed like this, I could actually talk to him.

I left for the party, almost convinced.

When I walked into the room, I put on my peacock-feather mask and caught a glimpse of myself in the mirror. I looked as glamorous as any drag queen there, yet I nervously downed two vodkas in the first ten minutes. I should have felt wonderfully safe in my disguise, but I still grabbed a glass of champagne every time someone poured one. I ended up anticipating *his* arrival in a blissful blur, the alcohol strengthening my conviction that he would indeed show up.

Maybe it was just my buzzed mind playing tricks on me, but the night seemed to fall under the kind of spell that entices you to enter a realm too heady for everyday life. With monsters mashing around me, the grotesques wearing all the secret knowledge of the universe in their warped smiles—the men-as-women more beautiful than any actual woman on earth—I was almost enjoying myself, even without his presence.

Someone grabbed me from behind, pushing a pointed snout into my neck. I turned around and saw a figure slouched in a Dalmatian-skin coat, with a huge red-nose mask obscuring

the upper portion of his face and a messy wig disguising his hair—a sort of "Cyrano de Bergerac meets Cruella DeVille." He was teetering dangerously, a full martini glass sloshing all over the place.

"So where's Prince Charming? It's after midnight." J.C.'s unmistakable sneer issued from behind the disguise. I should have guessed.

I shot back a suitably sarcastic reply, but I was shaken. What if he didn't come after all?

As I was standing in the bathroom line, a tangible wave of depression hit me as strong as the earlier spell had. The Cure was screaming, *"Why can't I be you?"* while a nun and a prostitute made out in front of me. I didn't know what sex either of them were; I doubted if *they* even knew. J.C. was at my back again, hissing, "Come on," now patting his matching Dalmation-skin purse.

Suddenly the idea of beginning a life of drugs didn't sound so bad. I started to follow J.C. into the bathroom when I caught a glimpse of the only non-costumed figure in the entire room, sauntering up the stairs. He was only a silhouette from my vantage point, but it was a silhouette I knew by heart. It was *him.*

In one quick glance, our eyes met, and for a ridiculous alcohol-induced second, I felt safe in my disguise. Then he began heading toward me.

I suddenly became obsessed with examining the black artwork on the wall beside me. He kept getting closer until, like one of my dreams unfolding, he stopped in front of me.

I thought, how can I *live* a dream? This is just supposed to happen—how should I know what to *do*? So I turned away, figuring I had nothing to worry about. Who in his right mind would speak to such a strange-looking girl?

Apparently, *he* would.

"Somebody slipped me an invitation to this party," he said. "How can I find them in this sea of people do you suppose?"

I realized that this was finally it—the Moment—our meeting made real. My heart was going through a series of mini-attacks; I didn't trust my own actions. Suddenly, it was as if I was possessed by all the cool, collected performances of bygone glamour queens—a foreign case of blasé took over my body.

"Yeah, there only must be about a thousand people here . . ." I said, my voice like ice. ". . . but it shouldn't take you too long to figure it out."

"Do you know where I can get a beer?" he innocently asked.

"It's called the bar." My words hung malignantly in the air and didn't contain a shred of how I always imagined I'd be with him. He just stared at me as I felt shame rush blood to my masked face.

At that very moment, I wanted nothing more than to hear my own words coming out of my mouth. I wanted to drop the stupid act and let him in on my silly secret so we could laugh the whole thing off, but something inside just wouldn't let me.

I caught a glimpse of J.C. lingering beside me. My face lit up with false gaiety as I fell into J.C.'s arms. "Kiss me, it's my birthday!" I said much too loudly, dipping myself in a passionate tango move.

When I lifted myself up a moment later, *he* was gone. I did hear him mutter, "What's she on?" as he walked away, but I just stood there with that fake smile on my face under my mask, like I had planned the whole episode. I then waited until he was down the stairs and safely unreachable again before I ran after him.

The streetlights outside seemed much too bright as they illuminated the completely empty street. I didn't bother going back to the party. I walked home as a cold drizzle started.

I can't shake that dampness now. I've been sitting here on the edge of my bed, watching the turntable spin. You know, a time definitely comes when it's not fair anymore to expect someone to shovel through your fears. Veiled in whatever mask you choose, you always end up the monster.

When I got home last night (I went to that party which, unbeknownst to me, was a claustrophobic costume affair—I lasted all of ten minutes), there was a drunk girl sitting in front of my apartment door. Her shoes were off, her knees were pulled up to her chest and she was sobbing with her forehead pressed against them. As this has never happened before, I was caught off guard, not immediately sure what I should do.

I said hello and stupidly asked if something was wrong. She told me in a voice with a slight accent that she wasn't feeling well and that her boyfriend lived across the hall. I tried unsuccessfully to get him to open his door, but ended up helping her to her feet and into my apartment. Once inside, she apologized again and again for causing me trouble and, in between sobs, told me her story.

It seems she was at her cousin's where she got drunk on red wine, although she did try to sober up before leaving by eating some chicken. (?) She somehow managed to make it to my building where she got inside and up the stairs before collapsing in front of my door. She knew her boyfriend was at work but wanted to wait for him anyway. She couldn't call him because he would get angry, and she couldn't call her parents (yes, jailbait) because they lived all the way out in Queens, and besides, they had forbidden her from ever seeing him again. One last attempt to get the boyfriend's work number revealed the fact that if he got pissed off, he would beat her up—and, anyway, he told her last week that he never wanted to see her again. She had no friends to call and couldn't remember her cousin's address or phone number.

Great. Just a little late-night drama to further convince me that my life will never know peace.

By the time she spilled her whole story, it was three-thirty and I was no longer feeling helpful. I told her to lie down on the couch and she immediately fell asleep. I wrote a note to the boyfriend, telling him I had something of his, shoved it under his door, and drank a beer while watching this girl twitch in her sleep. Finally, at six, there was a pounding on the door and I heard someone mumble, "You got my girlfriend in there?"

I opened the door and pointed to the couch. He walked over, put her over his shoulder and carried her out, saying, "Thanks, man. I hope she didn't do anything too fucked up."

"No problem," I said, closing the door behind them.

For a few minutes I stood by the door, listening for signs of domestic violence, but heard nothing. Finally I went to bed, exhausted, but for some reason I was unable to sleep.

I feel like hell.

I woke up with absolutely no idea of where I was. The room was totally dark, and the digital numbers on my clock read ten-thirty—it occurred to me that I must have slept all day, but I didn't know *which* day or why I'd done such a thing.

I switched on the lava lamp beside the clock and looked around this small room I've been living in for the past nine months, and *nothing registered.* Then, as if my body were awakening even more slowly than my mind, I sensed something constricting my thighs, which turned out to be my glorious dress, twisted tightly around my legs. At first, I didn't even recognize it—my only thought was, "Why am I sleeping in a dress?" Not "*the* dress," but "*a* dress."

I then felt a wave of nausea beginning to rise from the bottom of my stomach. I ran to the bathroom and my memory returned with it—just as unwanted.

Now I'm lying here on this skinny excuse of a futon that I swear has lost the little padding it once had, examining the rip in the side seam of my dress that I didn't notice until this very minute. When did it happen? While I was wrapping myself up like a mummy in my sleep? Or was it there for everyone to see at the party, to add to my humiliation? As if anything could top what actually happened.

Something is very, very wrong here—and my lack of concern about a roomful of people seeing my midriff through a gaping hole in my dress is only the tiniest symptom of it. I seem to have a lack of concern for anything at all except this crazy dream in my head about some guy I don't even know. I keep spouting off these noble ideas about avoiding the bullshit in life and embracing the *real*—but I can't even approach him unless I'm hiding behind a mask or an accent or an anonymous invitation, and even then, I can't start a civilized conversation. How real is *that*?

What was I thinking, inviting him to a *costume* party of all things? Am I really so anxious to hide my identity while desperately yearning to find his? Or do I even *have* a self to hide? Maybe the costume and theatrics are just drapings to give shape to my otherwise formless existence.

My head is upside down and inside out, and it's not just from puking my guts out. For a while now, I think I've been questioning this born-again-Bohemian lifestyle of mine. It, like everything else, seems none too pure right now. Yuppiehood may have been a vacuum of the soul, but why should I expect Hippiedom or the "grunge" lifestyle, or whatever it's called, to better nourish my spirit? For that matter, who am I, anyway, to lament the spiritual condition of the human race? What the hell have *I* done lately that's contained even a molecule of this deepness I keep blabbering about? This great new life of mine has consisted of getting sloppy-drunk every night, with friends I'm not even sure I like—after completing the rewarding job of serving mediocre Mexican food to crabby customers. No wonder I trail around like a lost puppy after some guy I don't even know, waiting expectantly for my fabulous "real life" to start unfolding.

Guess what? This *is* real life, babe, and it's sure no fairy tale.

I'm wondering, as I write, if the heat emanating from the extension cord on which my feet are resting should be of concern to me. I can't recall ever placing my bare piggies on or even near an operating extension cord in the past, so I can't really say that this cord is much hotter than other cords I've been in the same room with.

It is possible, I guess, because of the lack of outlets and multitude of adapters which are crammed full of plugs sucking in energy from somewhere out there that maybe I'm flirting with an electrical catastrophe. I'm no scientist, though, so I probably should just relax and warm my toes.

I've been thinking a lot lately, maybe too much. I remember when I was about ten years old, I got this idea in my head that I was a long-lost princess. I'd overheard Dad telling someone that our name translated from a Slavic dialect meaning "servers of the people"—kind of a royalty for the masses.

I tried to get my little sister Jeannie to bow down to me. (My impeccable child-logic conveniently dismissed the fact that she was my blood sister and therefore a fellow princess; it was so much more fun to think of her as a maid-in-waiting.) For some reason, she didn't find what I wanted her to do so fun. But I didn't care what she thought. I was so caught up in the lure of my fantasy that I was determined that it would come true.

Another day, we were playing at the edge of the woods, careful to keep the house in sight. We were playing "Little House on the Prairie." (I was the blind Mary, wandering farther and farther into the woods while Jeannie-as-Laura begged me to stay close to home.)

We were farther into the thick of trees than we'd ever been before, when she broke out of her role and called me by my real name. I stared at her blankly, still a blind girl with another name.

"C'mon," she pleaded. "We can't see the house anymore."

"I can't see *anything*." My voice was horribly icy and put-on.

"Stop it," she said. "You're not blind and you're not Mary."

I took full advantage of the moment. A wicked smile crossed my face as I switched roles.

"Of course not. You know who I *really* am, don't you?"

My face even *felt* unnatural as I grinned evilly at her.

"Stop it."

"I'm your beloved Princess, aren't I?"

Jeannie stubbornly shook her head.

"Bow down, maid, or I'll leave you to the wolves."

Jeannie continued to shake her head, but she was starting to choke up.

"Look into my eyes and you'll see it's true. These aren't your sister's eyes, but the eyes of a great Princess."

Jeannie's downcast gaze darted up at me, and I saw doubt and fear flickering in it.

"Bow down to me!" I commanded.

I shoved her face down hard into the soggy leaves, then ran away as fast as I could, ducking behind a nearby bush as she pulled herself up.

I watched her for a good ten minutes from my cover, watched as she turned in small, useless circles and called out my name in hiccupy sobs. At first she called my real name; then she sank to the ground and in a high, thin voice, she began to wail, "Princess . . ."

My Princess, help me!

I came out of nowhere to rescue her. I took her scared little form in my arms and rocked her, rocked her sobs away, rocked everything right again—see, I *was* the most wonderful princess in the world. I just *knew* I would be.

I'm no longer questioning the motive behind Randy's hiring me. The hands that in the beginning touched mine to guide the knife, continue to touch, but not necessarily just my hands. I've tried to let it be known that I'm not a touchy kind of person by saying things like, "That makes me uncomfortable," and I've walked to the other side of the butcher block, and just plain old ignored him.

That's all very clear to me, but Randy has shown no signs of getting my point.

It's not exactly voyeuristic, is it? It's just that all these windows from the backs of apartment buildings face me, and when I'm staring out at the dead winter gardens, hoping for a flash of color from a cardinal or a blue jay, any movement in a window sometimes catches my eye.

Like the window that is half-filled with a brown U-Haul box, bordered by a sliver of a dingy curtain. Someone stood today in the dark, remaining open space. His face was obscured by shadows, but the gray sunlight fully illuminated the white T-shirt he was wearing. It had three vertical panels, like a comic strip, with the pictures printed in black. From top to bottom, it was the progression of a huge ship sinking. But he was moving his body, slowly and steadily, up and down, so it appeared to be a primitive cartoon show from my perspective. I wonder if he knew this is how it appeared from the outside, or even if he was doing it intentionally, for some strange reason. Yet here *I* was, watching it, for no better reason.

In another window, at night, sometimes a light rapidly blinks on and off. It almost seems like a code, as if a frantic prisoner who is bound and gagged—yet somehow has access to the light switch—is trying to signal for help to the outside world. Or something shady . . . like a go-ahead for a drug deal . . . or the disguised "red light" of a prostitute. It gives me the creeps, but sometimes I try to time the intervals of dark between the flashing of the light, looking for a pattern. So far, there is none.

It's dusk now, and lights are appearing in the previously blank squares. Through a double window with no curtains or blinds, I can see a room clearly. The frame of the window seems the same size as the drive-in movie screen that was behind our house when I was growing up. Jeannie and I used to climb onto the roof of our clubhouse and watch the R-rated movies until Mom caught us. We always claimed we thought it was Disney.

Now, in this room, people are beginning to assemble. The TV is on, and they are gathering around to watch it. No one is wearing any clothing. A man leisurely stretches and walks to the window. He looks straight out at me, watching him. I'm sure he can't see me, but I begin to feel sick. Then he smiles, a gross little smile of acknowledgment.

I drop the edge of my curtain and walk quickly away, to the bathroom, where there are no windows.

I was out drinking earlier tonight, and I had this major flashback to when Lulu and I were kids. I remembered one time riding my bike to football practice and feeling like I was peddling straight toward hell, when I saw Lulu sitting in the school parking lot. She was sitting all by herself on one of those cement parking bumps, just looking at her feet. I remember wanting to stop and sit with her more than anything else in the world. I didn't, of course. Instead I went to practice and hated it more than I ever thought possible. The whole time I kept thinking about my sister. I wondered what she was doing and if she was still there. I hoped she was having a better time than I was.

I had that same exact feeling tonight. The bar seemed like it was smothering me—all the faces in it constantly looking around the room as if tonight they were going to find some kind of answer, some salvation. I thought of Lulu and I hoped that she was anywhere in Bloomington except a bar.

Suddenly the whole idea of anyone trying to find peace of mind at the bottom of a beer bottle in a roomful of people as drunk and scared as themselves seemed so fucked up. How many years have I spent drowning my insides, hoping (I suppose) to drown my heart and wash away the chance for anything real or true?

The world used to be easier to deal with in soft focus, but now it takes three times as much stuff to convince me I'm having a good time and three more days afterwards to pick up my ass and get on with my life.

I left the bar thinking I would call Lulu tonight, but when I got home, I changed my mind. I wrote her a letter instead, and told her that I loved her and that I wished the world for her. I asked her to say a prayer for me, or at the very least, to call the radio station and dedicate a song to me. She's going to think I'm the best flipped-out brother a girl could ever have.

Crazy Times

The following is a previously unpublished letter, dated Nov. 12, 1959, from the psychologist C. G. Jung to Ruth Topping, a prominent Chicago social worker. ——————————— in a comment of his in a Chicago newspaper: "Among all my patients in the second half of life ... every one of them fell ill because he had lost ——— the living religions of every age have given their followers, and none of them has been really healed who did not regain his religious outlook." In her letter, Miss Topping wondered how Jung would define the phrase "religious outlook."

By C. G. Jung

ZURICH

When you study the mental history of the world, you see that people since times immemorial had a general teaching or doctrine about the wholeness of the world. Originally and down to our days, they were considered to be holy traditions taught to the young people as a preparation for their future life. This has been the case in primitive tribes as well as in highly differentiated civilizations. The teaching had always a "philosophical" and "ethical" aspect.

In our civilization this spiritual background has gone astray. Our Christian doctrine has lost its grip to an appalling extent, chiefly because people don't understand it any more. Thus one of the most important instinctual activities of our mind has lost its object.

As these views deal with the world as a whole, they create also a wholeness of the individual, so much so, that for instance a primitive tribe loses its vitality, when it is deprived of its specific religious outlook. People are no more rooted in their world and lose their orientation. They just drift. That is very much our condition, too. The need for a meaning of their lives remains unanswered, because the rational, biological goals are unable to express the irrational wholeness of human life. Thus life loses its meaning.

Loss of faith, loss of meaning.

That is the problem of the "religious outlook" in a nutshell.

The problem itself cannot be settled by a few slogans. It demands concentrated attention, much mental work and, above all, patience, the rarest thing in our restless and crazy time. □

J.C. keeps asking why I don't want to go out anymore. What am I supposed to tell him—that it wasn't really me who spent all that time with him, but my evil twin? He keeps asking, "Well then, what do you want to *do*?"

Two girls from Amsterdam called me tonight, and I couldn't even bring myself to offer to meet them. They sounded disappointed—what the hell is Izzy doing, telling all those people at the Raven about me?

I'm sitting alone in my bright white room, wondering. White and silent because that's all I can bear right now. Wondering what all of us are *doing* here in this city, caught up in our glamour fantasies that barely disguise the wanderings of sad ghost-children looking for a home.

I'm wondering what ever happened to those silhouette cutouts of our profiles that Mom made for us when we were kids. Now it feels like all that's left of mine is the paper the form was cut from—with a big hole where the image of me should be.

I'm remembering my first trip to the zoo and how I was so disappointed that the polar bears were a dingy *yellow* color; I had always imagined them to be snow white. Why does it seem like nothing real has ever been as good as it is in my head?

Earlier, on my way to work, a bird literally died at my feet. It just fell from somewhere and landed in front of me, still twitching. I'm not thinking it's an omen or anything, but it did make me wonder why I'm still going through these same motions.

I scooped up the bird with a piece of cardboard and took it to the empty lot on 11th Street with the words *decent burial* running through my head like a mantra. I dumped it over the chain-link fence and stared at it a long time.

That big old Plymouth is still for sale. I took down the number, but there was no answer when I called. I don't know why I called, exactly. I've never wanted to own a car before (although I have thought at times that a motorcycle would solve all my problems).

There's just something about this car. It's so ridiculously large and it looks like the perfect getaway vehicle. I imagine myself taking off with a lover, heading out West, honking as we drive through our respective hometowns. Not stopping until we reach Big Sur, where we pull over, get out, and have swashbuckling sex on the hood as the sun sets over the end of the world.

Lord help me.

My phone rang at ten-thirty this morning. Not so early, I guess, but since I've been skipping shifts at the restaurant, I tend to sleep in longer. Go figure that one.

I almost didn't answer, but my still-asleep mind seemed to be under the impression that this could be the one phone call that could change my life . . . and what if I missed it?

"Hello?" I was so groggy that I must have sounded hostile, because there was a long pause at the other end before a guy's voice hesitantly said my name.

"Yeah?" I replied, in a "so what if it is?" tone.

"This is Harold."

Who?

"Uh, I don't know if you remember me or not. We met last winter, on Second Avenue. I found your bank card."

"Again?" I was so confused; I remembered the homeless guy now, and how stupidly I had met him, alone in the middle of the night. You can bet I'd never do that now—I mean, look where it got me. Here it was almost a year later and he was still calling me, no doubt to ask for an increase in his reward.

"I don't do that anymore," I said. "I don't meet strangers in the middle of the night. I've been reading the papers since I last saw you."

"It's ten-thirty in the morning," he said reasonably. "And I'm not *technically* a stranger since you met me once."

"What did you find this time?" I asked wearily, all too aware that lately I *have* been losing things all over the place.

"Come meet me at the same spot and I'll show you."

He hung up and I dragged myself off the futon, cursing his presumption that I would, in fact, go meet him. I was pulling a sweater over my head when I decided that nothing I could have lost was more important than warm blankets, and I crawled back under them.

The phone rang again later.

"At least I'm not calling collect," he said.

This was true.

"Okay, okay, I'm coming," I grumbled. It was beyond my control at this point. It was like I had to finish playing out a role I'd created ten months before.

Outside, the sun was magnificently bright in the way that it can be only in icy air. It stung my face but I didn't feel cold, only the burning of the wind.

I turned the corner to Second Avenue and there he stood, waiting, in the exact spot as last time.

"Harold," I said. "Have you moved?"

"Yeah!" He misunderstood my bad joke. "That's what I wanted to tell you. I've got a place now."

This wasn't what I expected.

"You look different," he peered closely at me. "You okay?"

Neither was this.

"This is the cab I'm driving." He indicated one of those brand-new strangely shaped yellow cabs. "I'm doing all right now."

"I'm . . . glad for you," I finally managed to say. "Really. It's great."

"I *knew* it was just some hard luck I was having," he rambled on enthusiastically, sounding like a high-school motivational speaker. "I *knew* things would turn around—things *had* to."

"Or else . . . ?" I said.

"Hey," he said sharply. "Don't go getting crazy on me. Don't let your head get into that shit. You just get it right out of there."

"Okay," I said in a tiny voice. I meant it.

"Listen," he said, a little embarrassed. "I just wanted to pay you back—I always thought of every penny I got as a loan. Of course, I didn't have *every*one's phone number."

We both smiled a little.

"Here." He handed me a twenty that wasn't all that new, but was impeccably pressed flat. I swear he must have ironed it.

"Thank you, Harold."

"Thank *you*."

We could have gone on all day like that, I'm sure, but someone came along who needed a cab, and I decided maybe I'd get cleaned up and swing by the restaurant. Maybe I could pick up a couple of my shifts that I'd left up for grabs.

I left work early today. At around nine-thirty, I'd say. No sooner had I walked in the door than Randy was commenting on how nice my shirt was, and sliding his hand down my back, resting it on my ass. As usual, every muscle in my body tensed as I shuffled around, looking for a place to put my coat.

"Busy day?" I asked.

"Oh, yeah . . . busy," Randy said as he put his fingers through my belt loop.

Again, I shifted my position, then mumbled something about having to go to the bathroom—a move I thought would enable me to put some distance between myself and the man with a thousand fingers. I shouldered my way past Randy and headed for the bathroom, the whole way hearing his voice behind me. I switched on the light and went to shut the door, when I felt a pull from the other side. Randy had followed me to the bathroom, and as far as I could tell, he thought I'd have no objection to his joining me there.

Like an explosion, I pushed my way out past him, knocking his glasses to the floor. And all I could hear was my voice yelling and the sound of the door banging into the wall as I flung it open to leave.

I ran down the stairs, leaving Randy at the top with his mouth open and his eyes wide.

The weirdest thing happened today. I'm pretty sure I shouldn't even try to tell anyone about it.

I was sitting on a bar stool at work; it was one of those endlessly slow days. J.C. and Nick were talking, not exactly excluding me, but it was no conversation I felt like joining. I was tracing cigarette burns on the bar with my fingertip, kind of connecting the dots.

Out of no particular thought, I suddenly saw myself sitting there on that wobbly bar stool, like you see yourself in dreams—you know it's "you," but you're somehow on the out-side, observing your actions from above.

Only what I saw didn't look like the "me" in mirrors or in pictures; what I saw was a very big, very old black woman, just sitting there with her eyes half-shut, barely rocking back and forth to the song she was humming in her head.

I knew there was a song in her head because it was *my* head, and I could hear it. It was a made-up Broadway musical–type tune. I knew she had come to this point where she was today, contentedly sitting at the Beach Grill Bar after struggling all her life, because I *remembered*—it had been *my* life. I felt the peace of where she was, the peace of not caring about anyone's opinion of her except her own. I knew she was now free of worrying about what others thought about her, because *I* had lived all those years of emancipation.

She turned ever so slightly, and opened her eyes a fraction of a crack; I saw that they were brimming. I knew those tears (of joy, as much as anything else) were a permanent and natural part of her. She smiled and nodded a little, more to the tune in her head than to react to anything around her.

Then J.C.'s sarcastic voice interrupted my daze.

"Look who's weepy again," he said.

I stuck my tongue out at him.

I'm not about to apologize for these tears anymore.

It's twelve-thirty, and I'm sitting on the steps of the post office. I've been walking around since eight, and just now the batteries in my Walkman are running low and it's causing Leonard Cohen to sound more pained than usual. So here I sit, staring at Madison Square Garden, trying to figure out my next move. I've spent the morning retracing the steps I've taken since I've been in New York. I feel like Ebenezer Scrooge, reliving my past in some desperate attempt to save my future. The Thai restaurant I used to work at is now a Pasta Express, and the first building I lived in is no longer there. Well, part of it is there, but most of it has burned to the ground.

I liked living in that apartment. I found it through the want ads, and the woman I lived with was a very un-funny stand-up comedian. I lived with her for about a year, and then she married some guy I never met and moved off to Connecticut, never to be heard from again.

Which is the way everything seems to have gone for me here. I've met and left behind more people and situations than I want to remember. And after yesterday, Randy is the freshest name on that ever-growing list.

I was fucking pissed when he followed me into the bathroom. It was the last straw, to be sure. But what's really too much is that when I woke up this morning, I felt that what had happened was somehow my fault. And to be fair, I guess that in a way, Randy's treating me like Anita Hill *was* my fault. Not that I was asking for it—no way. But I knew the truth long before yesterday, and still I stuck around, hoping like a child that it would all go away.

But where does that leave me now? This impromptu

trip down memory lane has only served to show me that my entire time in this city has been spent shuffling around from job to job, apartment to apartment, like some demented foster child trying to find . . . what? And now here I sit on the steps of the post office, hoping for something to happen.

J.C. and I were pelted tonight walking home from work.

He had been arguing with me that miracles are passé now, and maybe they didn't even exist in the first place. I said I was sure they are still around, but are just of a quieter, everyday variety now.

"If they're supposed to make people believe," he said, "they should be as big and flashy as possible."

"I think the idea is to believe before they happen," I said. "Otherwise you might miss them altogether."

We were passing in front of a brightly lit, fifties-style café when the first round hit. All around us the air filled with flying objects, hitting the ground, hitting the window, hitting *us*. We pressed ourselves against the huge plate window, our arms instinctively covering our heads, having no idea which way to run in order to escape this unexpected assault. I caught a glimpse of a diner on the other side of the window; his face stared out at me in horror. I looked down at my white sweater—it was covered with blotches of red.

I felt no pain, but I didn't trust my senses, which seemed to be working independently of each other. I was aware only of a strange, overriding sensation that gradually registered olfactorily: a strong, sweet smell.

"Hey," I said in amazement, "they're *strawberries*."

Then I could see the bright red fruit crushed all around us, along with several of their green cardboard pint containers. A new batch fell, thrown from somewhere up above.

We backed away from the window, joking and laughing in relief. We even did a sort of dance among the falling fruit while the patrons of the restaurant openly stared at us, a safely sealed-away audience.

"I've been hit!" J.C. howled, clutching at a red stain near his heart and staggering dizzily around. Our giddy exhilaration filled the space where the earlier fear had left an impression.

"Man, were we ever lucky," I said as we finally walked away from the scene.

"Lucky!" J.C. exclaimed. "This was a new jacket."

I tried to point out that in this city, it's bullets that usually pelt innocent bystanders, and acts of violence aren't always so sweet-smelling, but J.C. just complained that this crap got in his hair, "and it even looked *good* tonight."

I can't believe he really missed it altogether.

Today I was walking past the schoolyard on 11th Street—it was recess and there seemed to be a thousand voices screaming and yelling to one another. I was walking along the fence, enjoying this break from the madness of my grown-up world, when I saw two boys no older than eight chasing another boy of about the same age. Their game didn't mean that much to me until I heard one of the chasers yell out, "Fag! You faggot!"

I stopped. All that I was enjoying about this playground situation disappeared. I stood by the fence and watched the three boys run off to the far side of the playground, shouting, "Faggot! Faggot!" until they were too far away for me to hear. I looked around at the other kids doing whatever they were doing, but the feeling I had had earlier was gone. I was no longer envious of those kids and their innocence, because the truth is, they aren't at all innocent. Already their minds have been poisoned with hate, and the sick fact is it will only grow as they do.

I was suddenly back in grade school playing Smear the Queer, thinking the game was all about me. I remember feeling different from the way I was supposed to and being scared shitless that everyone could tell. When I came to New York, I thanked God for a place where, if being gay wasn't totally accepted, at least it was tolerated. But who the fuck wants to go through life being "tolerated"? Who the hell wants to spend their life being careful?

It's amazingly sad in New York tonight. This city was

the one place I thought I could come to and feel even the
smallest amount of security and freedom—but today, in one
instant, it was all blown away by a group of eight-year-old
kids on a playground.

I saw *him* today, through the window of one of those old-timers' barber shops.

The sun was glinting off the scissors that were cutting his hair, and a white vinyl cape shimmered around him. Amazingly, I wasn't seized by the old heart-pounding paralysis anymore. Instead, I stopped and looked straight at him, half expecting him to crawl under the sink at the sight of me. Instead, he smiled.

Maybe it's true that once you've faced a fear it can no longer haunt you—at any rate, I found myself walking into the shop, past the heavy, raised eyebrows of the barber, to stand next to him. In the mirror, I looked his reflection right in the eye.

"I want to apologize," I said. "*I* was the one who invited you to that costume party."

He started to speak, but I stopped him before he could make it easier on me.

"I know I wasn't very nice, but it's hard to be yourself when you're being someone else."

He swiveled to the side in his chair and looked into my *real* eyes.

"It's nice to finally really meet you," I said.

Then the barber sighed and asked if I would be finished anytime soon, like maybe by Christmas? I realized, in fact, that I *had* finished something, so I headed toward the door.

"See you around," I said to him.

A lock of hair slipped from the scissors and slid to the pile of dead ends on the floor.

I glided out of the shop, free at last, and into the light.

Idea #4

A new perfume for middle America: White Trash.

Slogan: "You know what you are. Now smell like it.

White Trash, available at finer drug stores everywhere."

Note: Got a haircut. Abomination.

Life's a real trip.

Here I am on the subway, feeling more than a little like I did on my first day in New York. After weeks of not going anywhere, I'm finally moving again. Hopefully right into the brownstone apartment I'm on my way uptown to see. It's way out of the price range of my minuscule tips, but maybe it's time I traded in my waitress apron anyway. I ended up stuck in limbo because I refused to go back to my old life, but why didn't it ever occur to me that I could go *forward*? Isn't it possible that some things have finally sunk into this image-soaked brain of mine? Am I not different? Or am I simply giddy now at the magical sight of a silver blur hurtling by the window on the other track?

"Follow your bliss," flashes through my mind. That's all I want, I realize, as I sit here on the old number one train, scrawling with a stub of lead in this now not-so-blank book. I feel just like Buddy Glass (or was it Zooey who liked to write in pencil?), since all of my pens have mysteriously disappeared. Lately, I've developed the annoying habit of losing everything I touch. I suppose this should be the cause of some concern (premature Alzheimer's?), but I've never felt more carefree. *Follow your bliss.*

It makes me want to laugh out loud—very loud—or maybe just tell the guy who's sitting across from me. He got on the train at the last stop, with a big travel pack slung over one shoulder. I looked at him in the first place because of that backpack; otherwise I probably wouldn't have noticed how his eyes suddenly welled up with tears as he stared out the now-darkened windows. Right out of the blue—he didn't look sad or upset or anything—tears appeared. The whole way that he contained them made me understand he was carrying something inside him, something he was perhaps long accustomed to, but which still sought a way out.

I really wish I could speak to him, even to make some inane comment like, "It will be all right," or "I know how you feel," but as I look at him again, I realize he doesn't need that reassurance. He looks so brave all of a sudden. He looks so *real.*

Now I guess I'd rather tell him about the lyrics on the post-card I got from Greggor and Annka—"Blowin' in the Wind," as translated back to English from Polish. I like them better than the original English, although J.C. finds the existence of a parallel set of English lyrics impossible.

I don't. Somehow they mean more, if only because hearing the unexpected makes you listen differently.

> *"How many ways must everyone go*
> *before we are human inside?*
> *How much water must the white bird fly over*
> *before she's on the other side?*
> *The wind knows the answer.*
> *The wind knows the answer."*

Hey, boy!

> *"The answer is all in the wind."*

I woke up this morning with the thought that today stood a very good chance of being dangerously similar to yesterday and the day before and most days that I can remember. As I was digging around for nickels and dimes to buy a coffee, I asked myself, "What the hell is going on?" and found that after several minutes I couldn't give myself an answer.

Suddenly I was flying around my room, throwing on my clothes, and ten minutes later I was on 9th Street, the proud owner of a car older than myself. So I've paid three hundred dollars for something which looks as if it's my last chance at getting out of here with half a mind. And although to anyone else it might seem a questionable investment, to me it feels all too right.

All I can see when I close my eyes is me and this lazy cat flying down the highway with the music up and the windows down. Like the song says, *"Freedom's just another word for nothing left to lose,"* and that is exactly the way I felt this morning when I opened my eyes and found them staring at a cockroach on the wall.

So it's good-bye to this apartment, and into the trash with most of my junk (though I am taking my tapes and my copy of *Where the Wild Things Are* to keep me company as I drive to who knows where). Wind and openness are what I desire today, and if it's just another silly idea, fuck it.

This car is going to take me somewhere I've never thought of going before, and if it's all the same when I get there, I'll head off in another direction. And if I'm running away from something, I guess I'll be all right as long as it never catches up to me.

I'm tired of messing up in the same big place, man, so now, like Jack, I'm on the road.

Wheels of Change

A recent study by the Council on Domestic Travel and Tourism shows cross-country travel by automobiles is on the upswing. Roadtrips for pleasure declined drastically in the 1980s when "super saver" airfares peaked in popularity even among students and lower-income travelers who typically rate travel by automobile as their number-one choice.

The recent surge in car trips is attributed to both economical and practical factors: Apparently, more Americans are now interested in seeing what lies between them and their destinations, with an astonishing 12 percent of travelers having no destination in mind at the onset of their trips.

What are the sociological ramifications of this trend? New York travel agent Susan Purdy says, "I like to think a new spirit of adventure has been injected into the tired veins of America. Either that or there are some awful good tire sales going on."

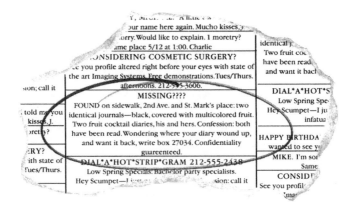

Y, ... A little ...
 our name here again. Mucho kisses, y
.orry. Would like to explain. 1 moretry?
ame place 5/12 at 1:00. Charlie

CONSIDERING COSMETIC SURGERY?
..e you profile altered right before your eyes with state of
the art Imaging Systems. Free demonstrations. Tues/Thurs.
afternoons. 212-555-3606.

MISSING????
FOUND on sidewalk, 2nd Ave. and St. Mark's place: two
identical journals—black, covered with multicolored fruit.
Two fruit cocktail diaries, his and hers. Confession: both
have been read. Wondering where your diary wound up,
and want it back, write box 27034. Confidentiality
guarenteed.

DIAL*A*HOT*STRIP*GRAM 212-555-2438
Low Spring Specials. Bachelor party specialists.
Hey Scumpet—I ...... sion: call it

sion; call it

told m. you
kisses, J.
oretty?

:RY?
ith state of
Tues/Thurs.

identical j.
Two fruit co.
have been read.
and want it bac

DIAL*A*HOT*S
Low Spring Spe
Hey Scumpet—I ju
infatua

HAPPY BIRTHDA
wanted to see y
MIKE. I'm so
Same

CONSID
See you profil
ma